Picket asked, "You looking for anything special?"

"The usual. A baseball bat with blood on it. The killer's wallet with his picture in it. You know."

Picket took out the picture of the dead man lying as Eliza had found him, facedown on the floor. He studied the photograph for a long time, then put it on the seat of a chair and began to look around.

"I can't see anything unusual," he said to Wilkie.

"Outside?"

Outside, stove wood was stacked on the deck of the porch, as always.

"So he opened the door to a caller, turned around, and got clobbered."

"With what?" Pickett asked.

"Something heavy, round and smooth."

Pickett said, "He was hit with a piece of two-inch oak dowelling about two feet long."

Wilkie grinned. "Now just tell me the color of the villain's eyes, his height, which leg he limped on, and I'll have him picked up this afternoon."

But Pickett was looking at the photograph again. "He could've been waiting. Inside."

ERIC WRIGHT

DEATH OF A HIRED MAN

WORLDWIDE®

TORONTO • NEW YORK • LONDON
AMSTERDAM • PARIS • SYDNEY • HAMBURG
STOCKHOLM • ATHENS • TOKYO • MILAN
MADRID • WARSAW • BUDAPEST • AUCKLAND

DEATH OF A HIRED MAN

A Worldwide Mystery/March 2005

First published by St. Martin's Press LLC.

ISBN 0-373-26521-2

Printed in U.S.A.

For Michael and Terry Paling

ONE

THE CALL CAME IN to the Sweetwater detachment of the Ontario Provincial Police about five minutes after Sergeant Abraham Wilkie and Constable Brendan Copps had arrived to begin the day shift. The duty officer listened for a few moments, then swiveled around in his chair to catch Wilkie's eye and repeated for the sergeant's benefit what he was hearing:

"Homicide, you think. Larch River. Adult male, unidentified. What's that? Identified. You know him. What's the address? Duck Lake Road, about a mile from the town. Log cabin on the south side of the road. There's a mobile home on the site, too? You live there. Right. Gotcha. Are you okay, ma'am? That's good. Stay there, don't let anyone on the property except one of us. We'll be there right away."

He put down the phone and looked up at the sergeant, who was staring at him, his hand held out for the message. "Put out to all patrols?" the officer asked.

"What?" Sergeant Wilkie read the message, frowning. "What?" he said again and stared back at the message. Finally he focused on the duty officer. "No. No. Yeah. No. Send some cars. Block the road at each end. Tell them we're on our way. Brendan!"

Constable Copps looked up, surprised, from the

cup of coffee he was pouring himself. "Us? Now?" He lifted his cup to indicate there were other priorities. First things, like coffee, first.

Wilkie shook his head, took down Copps' parka from the hook where Copps had just hung it, threw it to him and took down his own. It was too early in April to be outside long without proper insulation.

"Why us?" Copps asked as he shrugged himself into his parka. "What's the red flag for?"

Wilkie thrust the message at him, slightly dramatically. "Read that. Out loud."

Copps read it slowly and handed it back. "So? Old guy in a cabin been mugged. We've still got time for breakfast."

"We'll pick you up a doughnut at the Open Kitchen."

"I'll need *something*. I came straight out this morning. No juice, nothing. I figured I'd get a cruller soon as we signed in. I was just about to ask you if you wanted one. They make 'em fresh every hour over at Donut Heav'n."

"Shut up about your goddam stomach for a minute, will you? You just finished reading the report; didn't it say something?"

"Not to me."

"An older guy in his sixties lives in a cabin a mile out of Larch River?"

"Oh, yeah. Right. The retired Metro cop who figured out that bake-shop murder. Right? Him? You knew him, didn't you?"

"Mel Pickett, formerly Sergeant Pickett of the Toronto police. *Jesus Christ!* We should have found those punks before this. Come on, let's buy you some goddam crullers so we can get going.''

WHEN COPPS CAME OUT of the diner, Wilkie had control of himself. "Sorry," he said as they were rolling down the highway. "Pickett started out with my dad. Did you know that? And he did help us figure out that case. He figured it out before we did."

"We'd have got there pretty soon. We knew what was going on. All we had to do was wait."

"We knew what was going on, but we goddam well did not know *where* it was going on, did we, until Mel Pickett showed us? It was Pickett who knew where the guy was hiding, not us. Remember?"

"It was the town cop who knew first."

"That's right. Everybody except you and me, the official investigation team. They all knew. So now Mel Pickett's dead, killed by a guy we should have nailed a month ago."

"Easy, Sarge, easy. Who is this we should have nailed?"

"The punk who's been breaking and entering around here lately, especially around Larch River. You answered some of the calls."

"I figured it was a couple of kids. You did, too, last time we talked."

"So I did. And we were going to have a look around one of these days, weren't we? Now it's too late. Now they've killed someone. Mel Pickett. You still think it was kids?"

"It doesn't sound like a real thief."

"What's a real thief sound like, for Chrissake, in this backwoods? Someone who kicks in the barn door and steals the chickens? There are no pros around here. No safecrackers. You can't crack a safe with a fucking pitchfork, can you? Christ, where are all these cars going?''

Copps waited for a straight stretch of highway so he could sip his coffee in safety. ''Abe, don't jump on me every time I open my mouth. What I meant is, a real thief, even here in the boondocks, is someone who's interested in thieving, not in mugging and raping and stuff like that. Even in Larch River, punks looking for jewelry and cash and stuff wouldn't go in with a baseball bat. And these cars, by the way, are just the locals going to work. Switch the flasher on.''

Wilkie switched on the flasher and the siren and put his foot down. The line of traffic shifted respectfully to the right to let him by.

''We don't know what he used. Maybe the crowbar he broke in with. Okay, so it sounds like a thug. My old man and Pickett were in Homicide together.''

''You told me, I think. Long time ago?''

''Fifteen years.''

''Then what?''

''My old man? He came off the street, got himself a quiet job in the courthouse.''

''And this Pickett guy?''

''The name is *Mel Pickett*. Okay?''

''Sorry. So what happened to him before we met him? I never spoke with him while we were on the case.'' Copps tried to find something that Wilkie could talk about, something to let some of the tension out.

''He worked in the Bail-and-Parole Unit. He could've retired, but his wife died and I think he was taking his time. They didn't have any kids, and apart from fixing up his house in Toronto, he didn't have a lot to do. Then he got a notion to build this log cabin. He found this site in Larch River and bought an old log cabin from an Esso dealer up near Bancroft. The guy was expanding and needed the space, so Pickett had the cabin taken down and shipped to his site, where he reassembled it.''

"He didn't really build it, then?'' Copps made himself sound brightly interested in Pickett's cabin. The way Wilkie was driving, he didn't want to irritate the sergeant further. He wanted to distract him a little, have him ease up. The building of Pickett's cabin seemed like a good topic.

"That's what I said. He'd tried to start from scratch. He found a guy to sell him enough cedar logs, and he'd stripped them and stacked them to let them dry out over the winter, to season them. But when he came back up in the spring, someone had stolen the lot.''

Copps started to laugh, then stopped when Wilkie looked at him. Wilkie resumed: "So he'd nearly given up. Then someone told him about this Esso dealer with a log cabin he didn't want. So you could say he did build it, really. He had the total experience of building it, which was what he wanted.''

This was better. Now the needle was flickering around 140 kph. "Wasn't there a woman involved? Seems to me he had a kind of girlfriend. What's the right term when you're an old guy? Ladyfriend? Female companion? Old doll?''

"He isn't that old. But yeah, that's the right term. Girlfriend. I wonder where she is.''

"These old coots, retired for years, still ripping it off. You hear about that a lot these days. Didn't use to be that way, did it?" Copps thought a little more chat might help drain away the rest of Wilkie's anger.

"When?"

"When I was a kid. My grannie, like. Yours. Still, you don't know, do you? Maybe they were going at it like minks but they just didn't talk about it. That's probably the only real difference between then and now. So what happened next, to this old cop?"

"He married the girlfriend. She ran the lunch counter at Harlan's motel. They got married down in Toronto near Christmas."

"You invited?"

"I don't think anyone was, or my dad would have been. No, we both got one of those little cards saying it had happened."

"Were there any kids left over from previous marriages? Watch it. They're slowing down ahead, on the bend."

"My dad told me once that Pickett had an illegitimate daughter, no, *granddaughter*." Wilkie smiled slightly as what he was remembering took precedence over his concern for Pickett.

"How do you get one of those?"

"He had an illegitimate son by a girl he knew in England at the end of World War Two. The son had a daughter, and when she grew up, when she was about eighteen, she got curious about her Canadian grandfather and came looking for him, and found him. Pickett and the kid got along well, and Pickett took her in for a while. In fact, I think she lived in his house in Toronto for a couple of years before she went back. That's what I heard.''

Copps swallowed the last of his cruller and started in on a jelly doughnut.

''How come you didn't have any breakfast?'' Wilkie asked. ''Don't tell me you slept by yourself last night. Don't they make your breakfast?''

''Marigold was pissed off with me about something. I came out of the shower, she's still lying in bed. I thought maybe she wanted me to join her for a quickie, you know—brekkers, like nooners—but it turns out she's just mad at me for getting up so early and waking her up, because she doesn't want to get up herself. But I had an hour's drive to work, and by the time she and I got sorted out, I had to be on my way, so I left her there. Did Mel Pickett have any money?''

''The usual, I would think. A pension, some savings, and the property in Toronto as well as the cabin here. Pour some of my coffee in your cup so I won't spill it. Gimme the cup. Put a napkin around it, for Chrissake—it's red-hot.''

Copps did as he was told, carefully. ''That all goes to the wife now?''

''I guess so. I think he had a relative in Hamilton he never saw—a sister-in-law, I think. Here, take this off me. This is the best coffee in Sweetwater, you say?''

''I said they had the best doughnuts, not coffee. So there's your first suspect.''

''The wife?''

''No, the sister-in-law in Hamilton. She stood to collect, if this Pickett hadn't got horny in his old age.

Always something families have to watch for. She's probably been counting on inheriting a bundle. A bundle by Hamilton standards, that is. Now she's cut out.'' He sipped his coffee, then crumpled the empty cup in his fist and rolled down the window.

"Don't throw it out the window, for Chrissake. Somebody will see you and report us for littering.''

"I wasn't going to. I just need to clear my tonsils.'' He hoiked for several seconds, collected a gob and spat through the open window. "There.'' He rolled the window up and put the crumpled cup in the door pocket. "Now I'm ready to go. Christ, that air's chilly.''

"Who's Marigold?''

"She's where I was last night.''

"Where's that?''

"Peterborough. You know people in Peterborough?''

"No. This Marigold a steady?''

"Not really. I look her up once in a while, or she calls me. She likes to stay loose, like me.''

In the middle of his concern for Pickett, Wilkie felt a familiar twinge of resentment. Copps had a lot of women, it seemed to him, obtained in a variety of ways, even through want ads. Generally, though, he just seemed to acquire them by brushing up against them and having them stick to him, as if with Velcro, or so it looked to Wilkie. Right now Copps had at least three long-term relationships like the one with Marigold, each in a different town, women who were glad to see him for the night if he called ahead to make sure they were free. Apart from these, he was always on the lookout for a one-nighter.

It seemed to Wilkie that Copps kept the possibility of sex always in mind, like a Frenchman with one eye out for a Routier sign. Not that Copps talked much, and he never bragged about his girlfriends. His women were, in general, his friends, and he talked of them as such, respectfully. Thinking about Copps' life Wilkie realized now that he had never heard Copps speak slightingly of women in general, or attribute the flaws in any woman to her being a woman.

"How's Helen?" Copps asked now.

"She's all right, I guess." The constable, Wilkie knew, was just being polite, but in the context of a conversation about Copps' sex life, it was an insensitive question, liable to misunderstanding. For, as Copps knew, Wilkie could not say, most nights, how his wife was, since she spent most of her weeknights in Toronto and came home to Sweetwater only on weekends. Before Copps could ask again, Wilkie said, "She's staying in the city this weekend to help out with some dinner her boss's giving for a visiting fireman."

"The boss not got a wife?"

"Yeah, but she asked Helen to help out. Helen's good at organizing stuff."

"Uh-huh. Duck Lake Road ahead," Copps said, relieved that the destination was in sight. "Stacey's here already." He pointed to the Ontario Provincial Police car blocking access to the gravel side road. As they approached, the car moved enough to let them by and the driver waved.

"If the dinner ends early, she might drive up late tonight." With Copps, Wilkie had trouble talking about Helen, feeling that Copps probably regarded him as a nerd for putting up with her. He didn't want to get into it.

Copps said, "Easy now. This road is full of potholes. They haven't graded it yet this year."

"How far down is it? You remember?" Wilkie asked.

"Half a mile. There."

Another cruiser was parked by a gate in the fence that ran along the road, and an ambulance sat inside the gate, blocking any further access. The cabin lay fifty feet beyond the ambulance.

Wilkie leaned on his horn, and the ambulance moved enough to let them by and park. An OPP constable came out of the cabin and walked down to meet them. "Photographer's on his way," he said as the two men got out of the cruiser. "Nothing's been touched."

"Why is this ambulance blocking the path?"

"Abe, take it *easy*," Copps said quietly.

The constable stepped back from Wilkie's temper. "I told them to stop there, just in case you wanted to examine the ground for tire marks, something like that. I figured they could carry the body this far when you released it. I'll tell the driver to move it out now."

Wilkie took a breath and shook his head. "No, no, that's good," he said, forcing himself to nod approvingly at the good sense the patrol officer had shown. "I should have stayed out on the road myself. Sorry."

He stood by the car looking toward the cabin as Copps, who had started up the path, turned to wait for him. Wilkie continued to look around the site.

Copps made a sign to the other constable to leave them alone. He walked back a step toward Wilkie.

"I can do this, Abe," he suggested.

Wilkie nodded that he had heard, but made no move. Then he straightened up. "No, you can't," he said. "This is mine." They walked toward the cabin, and once more Wilkie stopped, this time on the porch steps. "This is my first time," he said.

"You never—" Copps began, amazed.

"They're all strangers, the ones we get on highway patrol. This is different. If you're lucky, you could go through your whole career without seeing the dead body of someone you knew, wouldn't you think?"

"Abe, let me do this."

Wilkie walked by him. "Let's get it over with."

The two policemen walked into the cabin, where the other patrol officer was waiting for them. The three of them stared at the body on the floor.

TWO

AT SEVEN O'CLOCK that morning, Mel Pickett and his wife Charlotte, accompanied by his small, foolish-looking dog, Willis, set out from Toronto on their way north to Larch River. It was too early in the year to worry about weekend traffic to cottage country—Larch River probably had one more big snowfall to come—but on Saturday mornings, Bathurst Street, the first part of their route, clogged up early with shoppers, and Pickett liked to get clear of the crowd before the stores opened.

"Where are we going to stop?" Charlotte asked as they crossed Lawrence on their way to the 401.

"Lindsay," Pickett said promptly.

"How far is that? How long?"

"Hour and a half."

She sipped at the mug of coffee she had brought from the house. "You want some of this?"

"I had two cups while you were putting on your girdle."

She looked out the window. "We'll have to work out a system," she said eventually.

"What for?"

"So I don't keep you waiting while I do what I have to do, not including putting on a girdle. When did you last see a girdle? I can't think straight with you standing by the window looking at your watch.''

''Just keen to get going, that's all.''

''And *I'm* keen to get dressed and drink my coffee in peace.''

He glanced over at her. She was looking ahead and smiling, but determined. She meant it. Not a quarrel, then, but another sorting out, some new rules to lay down. She was just carrying out her intention, long stated, of avoiding misery by announcing that it was coming. She would not harbor a grudge or nurse a complaint; she would speak as soon as the cause surfaced, before it became a complaint. That was the advice they had had.

''Next time, I'll know,'' he said.

She smiled at him properly now and stroked his thigh. ''There won't be a next time. You know now.''

''It'll be something else next time.''

''Me bothering you, probably,'' she agreed.

''I'll tell you if you do.''

''We're doing well so far, don't you think?''

''Yes, we are.''

They had been married for three months: he, a sixty-six-year-old retired policeman, a widower; she, a sixty-two-year-old widow, who most recently ran a coffee shop in Larch River, where Pickett used to drink coffee when he was building his cabin. They were on their way now to her house in Larch River, one of the homes they shared, and should by now have decided whether to sell it or keep it, but apart from the various sentimental attachments each had to house or cabin, the real-estate market was almost lifeless, and they could justify their procrastination by seeming to be waiting for better times, while in fact they were simply waiting to let the sensible decision reveal itself. They were in no hurry, after all. In their sixties, they had all the time in the world.

The marriage counselor they had consulted together and separately before they married had warned them that the property might constitute the biggest area of contention, but they had had no difficulty so far. Both of them had lived well within their individual incomes when they lived alone, and after they married and the costs were shared, they had even more money left over. So he continued to maintain his house in Toronto and his cabin and trailer in Larch River, and Charlotte kept her house. It was obvious to Pickett that their lifestyle would be adequately served if they kept his cabin and spent the good seasons in Larch River, and moved to his house in Toronto for the winter, with excursions to Florida and, for him, to England, a place he liked to visit ever since he had spent part of the war there with the Royal Canadian Air Force.

It was also obvious to Pickett that the idea of getting rid of her house would have to come from Charlotte, who, he assumed, like most women, was sentimentally attached to the place she had lived in for so long, and he would have to allow her to give it up in her own time. Another reason—so said the marriage counselor—was that Charlotte was trying to keep her head, and thus she insisted on bearing in mind the possibility that their marriage might not last, the statistics on the durability of October marriages being no better than on those contracted in May. And so she wanted to keep the house, just in case. Pickett received this opinion and judged it by where it came from, as the disillusionment of a professional watcher of the marital skies, now second-guessing her clients. Pickett was sure it did not apply to Charlotte, although it wasn't a thing you could ask her about.

The idea of consulting a marriage counselor before the marriage began instead of when it broke down was Charlotte's. The idea had appalled Pickett, but he had agreed to go along with it to the extent of consenting to a joint interview, with Charlotte present, and an individual one, without her. The counselor was a woman, and all of her training was directed toward getting people to see the source of their troubles; she'd had no experience in counseling people without any problems. She made an effort to explain to them something called "mirroring," a technique that as far as he could understand her, involved repeating back what your partner had just said until she agreed you had heard her right, apparently to show how you usually didn't. But so far, that wasn't a problem between them.

The woman had irritated Pickett immediately by telling him that she thought Charlotte a truly special person, shaking her head with amazement either that a woman who ran a diner should have her wits about her or that such a woman should want to marry someone like Pickett. Then she found a way of saying something comparable about him, embarrassing him with a paragraph of praise about his sensitivity, which he thought was bullshit, and then she made her point that each in their own way was so extraordinary that they would have to work hard to humor each other's uniqueness, a word she used several times, and now he understood she was saying that at their age, they were probably cranky and it was something they should keep in mind. She should just have pointed out that old people get crabby, so they should watch for it. He also didn't like the way she laughed, or that she laughed at all.

In his private interview, the counselor had concentrated, as Pickett had feared she would, on the problems he would have in bed. "She gave me a little pamphlet about all the ways they have to help me get it up," he told Charlotte. "Chemicals, pumps—*pumps!*—implants. If I use them all, we could do it twice a day."

They had been lovers for six months.

Charlotte said, "She didn't know. She was trying to be helpful. That's why we consulted a counselor, to see what might lie ahead."

"I don't need her help. Do I? What did she say to you? About sex?"

"She told me not to expect too much at first. Said I should be understanding. I am, aren't I?"

Much later, when he was over his embarrassment and irritation, they agreed that Charlotte's instinct had been sound, that at the very least, their vocabulary had expanded in a way that would make it easier to raise problems and, therefore, presumably easier to solve or avoid them. All the language of domestic and sexual problems had been set out, ready for use. They took no further counsel, feeling that premarital counseling for geriatrics was in an undeveloped state, but that wasn't the counselor's fault.

As they approached Whitby, Charlotte said, "Turn up to Greenbank. We could stop at the Chicken Coop and get some bread, too. I don't know where you buy bread in Lindsay."

She meant real bread, the kind Pickett had trained her to like, one of his small triumphs in their marriage so far. Once there had been good bread available in Larch River, but the bakery closed after the baker's brother was sent to prison for killing a man. Now the only available bread came sliced and wrapped in waxed paper.

As they turned off 401 on the road to Greenbank, she said, "Tell me again about this granddaughter of yours in England."

He had told her the story of Imogen early, told her lightly; then, when they started to think about wills, he had told her again. One of the things that had made it easy for them to make decisions about wills was that both were childless from their previous marriages, and they began thinking the situation through with the assumption that whoever outlived the other would inherit everything. After that, Pickett had explained, the survivor would make out a new will, leaving it to whomever he or she liked. Pick an heir.

"If I survive you," he had said, "I'll leave the lot to Imogen." Next to Charlotte, Imogen was the one who had given him the greatest pleasure since his wife had died.

It was at the end of the war," he said now. "I was stationed in England in the RCAF. I had a girlfriend, a WAAF, and she got pregnant. She didn't want to marry me—she thought it was unfair to me—so when her father kicked up a fuss, she and I agreed I should play the villain and refuse to marry her. Complicated, isn't it, but I was only nineteen. I thought I was being, you know…''

"Gallant. Would you have married her?"

"I'd have crawled across broken glass for her. Like I said, I was only nineteen.''

"So what happened?"

"Nothing. I came home. She had the baby. I got married to Mary eventually, and we didn't have any kids.''

"And you never saw the English girl again?"

"Sure. Whenever I went to England, like every seven or eight years. I'd arrange to meet her—Mary knew about it—just for a drink. A walk in St. James' Park. Something like that.''

"You still felt the same way? And Mary didn't mind?"

"No, how could I? I was a happily married man. But it was nice seeing her, sitting in the park, talking. I did all the talking, but that's the way she was.''

"Sounds to me like she still had something going for you.''

"Maybe. It didn't flare up, though, not when I was there.''

Gratitude, he thought. That's what she had still felt for him. For the baby was not his; he had returned to Canada a virgin, which was normal enough for the times.

His declaring himself the father and refusing to marry her had been more gallant than Charlotte knew, designed for him to take the blame, get her off the hook, and keep dark the existence of her real lover, a married art teacher in Croydon. No one else knew the story now that she was dead, and Pickett wondered if he would ever tell Charlotte. He was not yet sure of how she would react to the notion of a possible circumstance in which all her estate wound up in the hands not of Pickett's illegitimate "granddaughter," but of someone who was not even that, someone he was not connected to by blood at all.

"She came over, you said, this girl."

"She lived upstairs in the house for nearly two years. Then she went back to England to enter the university."

"And you want to leave her everything? Nothing to her father, your son?"

"I'm attached to her. I'd rather leave it to her than to anyone else. I never even met her father."

"What about those people in Hamilton?"

"My sister-in-law Verna? Okay, I might leave something for her son, Mary's nephew. He's been expecting something since he was in long pants. But I don't have any obligations to Verna."

"Won't she have expectations, though?"

"She might have had—no, she *did* have. But that was before she met Imogen. One day when she came to the house—she used to drop by every couple of months to remind me that her kid was my nephew and to learn if I planned on dying soon—anyway, one day she came and found Imogen there. That was just after Imogen arrived from England, when she had purple hair and a white face. I told Verna she was my newfound granddaughter, and the implications for her kid were so horrendous that old Verna just about lost it. She'd always been worried I might marry the librarian next door, but a kid of eighteen? She accused me of picking up Imogen on Jarvis

Street. So we had a knock-down, drag-out argument, which I kind of enjoyed because it gave me the excuse to tell her to go away and not come back.''

"She sounds to me like someone who won't give up easy.''

"Then she'll give up hard, because I don't intend to leave her a penny.''

"This Imogen. Did she remind you of her grandmother?''

"Yes, she did.'' Pickett returned to the topic of Verna. "I'll leave something for Mary's nephew. He's spent a long time expecting it, or his mother has, so it's not fair to cut him off completely. A few thousand, anyway.'' But nothing, he thought, for the blade-faced Verna, his sister-in-law. "Besides, it might stop them from attacking the will. Or that's what I thought before I met you.''

"You don't have to justify it. You want to leave him a bit of money, so go ahead. But you'd better check that out. I read somewhere that it's easier to attack a will for not leaving you enough than for leaving you out completely.''

They had both become aware that simply leaving everything to each other was inadequate preparation against, say, their dying simultaneously in a car accident, and they had begun to list other people they wanted to be remembered by, or to whom they felt responsible. So far, in case he died the next day, Pickett had made a temporary will leaving his property to Charlotte—she would inherit his pension automatically—and his money to Imogen. Charlotte left him her house and half of her money; the other half she mentally redistributed every day, but temporarily it was destined for her sister, whom she didn't get on with and whose husband owned a road-paving company and didn't need more money.

"Does Imogen know she's your heir?"

"Her father does, and I imagine he's told her. I wrote to him, telling him I planned to put Imogen in my will, but that I didn't want to be unfair. Imogen has a sister, see, and I could be leaving a nice little sum. So I wondered if I should leave it to him in trust for the two girls. But why not just leave the two girls half each?"

"What if I die first?"

"You leave your money where you like, and anything you leave to me, I'll put in the kitty for my granddaughters. Might even give my nephew a bit more."

"Let's see who dies first."

"That's it. Don't rush it. Gives us an interest in life, doesn't it?"

"Weren't you curious about your son?"

"No."

"Coldhearted swine."

"My lawyer says maybe I should adopt him."

"How old is he?"

Pickett did the sum in his head. "Late forties?"

"Your lawyer must be joking. You can't adopt someone that age, surely?"

"I don't see why not."

"If he's not joking, why would you?"

"He says that would make him my natural and legal heir."

"Are you going to?"

Pickett took a deep breath. "Yes," he said. "I'm going to try. I've written to him to suggest it."

"Dear God. Have you heard back?"

"Not yet."

All this was news to Charlotte, because until now, Pickett had felt shy of telling her. There was something slightly odd, if not silly, about adopting your own son, but the idea, once born, had refused to go away. It was, in fact, Pickett's idea, not his lawyer's, rising out of a conversation with his lawyer about whether his sister-in-law would have a claim on his estate. His lawyer's response was to the effect that they could not stop her from making a claim, and circumstances might make it plausible. Could Verna claim that her sister, Pickett's first wife, had made promises before she died? Did Verna by chance have any letters from her sister implying that bequests would be made?

One reason he hadn't told Charlotte the truth was that you couldn't trust an adult woman to understand how a nineteen-year-old boy had acted. And now that he'd found Imogen, he didn't want to take the smallest risk of losing her. Now once more he felt overwhelmed by a desire to confide in Charlotte, to share his secret, and to account for his strange wish to adopt his own son. He turned to her, preparing the first phrase.

She said, "I think that's a lovely idea. Like reconfirming your marriage vows."

He said, "I should have told you."

"Of *course* you should. Of *course* you should. But you wanted to surprise me. Anyway, you have to have some secrets. We all do. Let me know what he says, though.''

So the moment passed, and Pickett guessed it would not come again.

THREE

THE MAN WAS sprawled facedown where he had fallen, the top of his head and one temple sticky with congealed blood.

"He's been dead for a while," the patrol officer said. "So when the station told us you were on your way, I figured that for the sake of another couple of minutes, you could see for yourself how we found him."

"We know who it is," Copps announced. He cleared his throat.

Wilkie put his hand on Copps' arm to stop him from saying any more, then walked over to the window and leaned his forehead against it while the others waited. Copps moved to him, saying so only Wilkie could hear, "Leave it alone, Abe. I'll look after it."

Wilkie shook his head slightly without answering, then turned and took a long look at the body across the room. Two or three minutes elapsed before he lowered himself beside the body. He looked up at Copps with an expression of wonder.

"No, we don't," he said. "I don't know who this guy is, but he isn't Mel Pickett." Then he stood up and wiped the sweat from his hands on his pants. "So, let's get an identification. Who phoned in the report?'' He clapped his hands to get them all going again.

"A woman named Eliza Pollock. She stays in that trailer." The officer pointed through the door at the little house trailer parked on blocks on the other side of the small clearing. "She's over there waiting for us now."

"Is she all right?"

"Seems to be."

"Who is she?"

"A friend of the guy who owns the cabin, she says."

"Bring her over. Let's get started."

THE WOMAN WAITED out on the porch while the officer who had gone to fetch her came in and reported to Wilkie. "She doesn't want to come in if she doesn't have to," he said.

Wilkie looked over the policeman's shoulder and saw a woman in her mid-to-late twenties, dressed in a sweatshirt, jeans, and leather ankle boots. Her mousy hair was dragged back and held by a rubber band, creating a stubby ponytail about two inches long. Beyond her, three men were walking down the path from the road toward them: the doctor, a photographer, and another technician. Wilkie waited for them to arrive at the cabin, then spoke to Copps.

"Let's go back up to her trailer," he said. He moved out to the porch. "Sergeant Wilkie," he said to the woman, holding out his hand. "I'm in charge now. You okay?"

"Oh, yes. I'm used to this. Remember me?"

"What?"

From behind him, Copps said, "This lady is the one found the body of the guy who was killed on the trail, remember?"

"Now I do," Wilkie said. "Can we use your trailer, stay out of the way of these guys?"

She turned and led the way across the clearing to the aluminum steps of the trailer, opened the door and waved him inside. She waited for him to squeeze in before she closed the door behind him, creating maneuvering room so they could sit down at the table in the tiny kitchen.

"You mind doing this twice?" Wilkie asked. "I mean for now, just tell me what happened and later on, make a formal statement to the constable. That okay?"

She nodded, holding her arms at the elbows, waiting.

"You *sure* you're okay?" Wilkie's own crisis had passed, but it had left him aware that she might still be recovering. "It must have been something, seeing him like that, thinking it was Mel Pickett. It upset me when I heard who it might be. What made you go in?"

"I never thought it was Mel. God, no. I knew it was the man who was living there. Norbert Thompson. I couldn't remember his name when I called you people."

"Right, right, right." Wilkie nodded himself back to normal. "Tell me how you found him, what you were doing."

"I was tidying up from breakfast before I started work, and I noticed that Mr. Thompson hadn't appeared yet and the porch light was still on. He was normally out and about early. He's been clearing a patch for vegetables up behind the cabin.''

"What kind of work do you do?"

"I'm writing a book."

"A novel, like?"

"No."

"What kind?"

She took a deep breath and leaned back. "It's a social and cultural history of Larch River from its origins, about 1890 to today, based on the records that still survive of parish magazines, the theater club, the weekly newspaper, and on interviews with three families I've found who go all the way back to the first settlement, and on their records, letters, diaries, and other documents. Why do you want to know?''

Wilkie wanted to tell her that he didn't really need to know anything about her project, didn't give a hoot, actually; it was just that he was so relieved not to find Pickett dead that he was having trouble thinking of the right questions to ask her. He was babbling a little, being agreeable. He looked across the table at what she had been working on, evidently something official.

He leaned over, grinning. "You just finished writing that, what you just told me?"

"Yes, I did. I'm trying to get a grant to pay for some of the research, and I was in the middle of writing the application."

"This is like a hobby, then?"

"A labor of love. Can we get back to him?" She pointed across to the cabin.

Wilkie forced himself to look professional. "So what did you do when you saw the porch light on and no one around?"

"I walked over to see if he was all right, of course."

"You knew him, then?"

"Hardly at all. We were just neighbors."

"So you saw his porch light on, and you walked in to see why?"

"After I noticed the light, I looked for any other signs. There was no smoke coming out the chimney, so he hadn't lit his stove. It's still too early to go without heat. There's a little electric heater in the kitchen that will get you through breakfast, but if you want to heat the cabin, you have to light the woodstove. That's what living in the cabin is all about. Authentic."

"You know the cabin pretty good?"

"I know the cabin and Mel and Charlotte pretty good, yes. Mel and Charlotte are friends of mine. I got to know them last year."

"Because of the homicide? That body you found up in the bush?"

"That was part of it, but I already knew Mel. I was directing the Little Theatre's play a couple of years ago, and we became friends when he offered to be our stage carpenter. So when I decided to write this book, I asked him if I could borrow this trailer on weekends."

"Okay. Now what's this guy, Norbert Thompson, doing in the cabin?"

"Mel rented it to him a few months ago. Thompson used to live on a chicken farm up toward Donnington,

with his brother and sister-in-law. They got into dif-
ficulties of some kind, had a falling-out, and Thompson left and moved into town, as they call Larch River
hereabouts. He was only supposed to be here temporarily, until Mel and Charlotte decided what they
wanted to do about the property. I don't think he was
paying much rent, if any. Is Mel really a friend of
yours?''

"He was a buddy of my dad's.''

"But personal stuff? Does he talk to you about
that?''

"I never see much of him unless someone gets
killed.'' Wilkie tried for a laugh. "Maybe two or
three times a year. Why? What's the problem?''

"I guess it isn't too personal. You know Mel put
this trailer here and used it while he built the cabin?''

"That much, yes. But I never met him up here until
you found that body, and I never spoke to his wife
except across the counter of that diner she ran.''

"Charlotte owns her own house here, and Mel has
a house in Toronto, so when they decided to get married, they had four places to choose from, though I
don't think Charlotte would count this trailer. Anyway, they haven't quite decided which way to go, so
they haven't given any of them up yet. You know all
this?''

"I haven't spoken to him since last year. Where
are they now? At her house in town?''

"No, in Toronto probably, on their way up here. I
was talking to them last weekend about their di-
lemma. They've got to make up their minds. Charlotte's house has been standing empty since last
Christmas, but she's as fond of her house as Mel is

proud of his cabin. She's thinking of trying to rent it, so as to postpone the decision for a while. Mel is doing the same thing with the cabin.''

There was a knock, and the door of the trailer opened. Copps' head appeared in the doorway. ''About finished. Can I roll it up?'' His eyes rested on Eliza and he came all the way into the trailer while he waited for an answer.

Wilkie said, ''Yeah,'' and shuffled sideways out of the space behind the table. ''Did you identify Thompson?'' he asked Eliza from the doorway.

''I was never introduced to him as Thompson. I identified the man on the floor as the one I saw about the cabin the last couple of weekends, since I started to come up here—the man I believed to be living in the cabin with Mel's permission. I remembered afterward that Mel had told me his name was Norbert Thompson.''

''Good.'' Wilkie pushed past Copps, who was still looking at Eliza. ''Let us know right away if you decide to go back to Toronto,'' he said from the doorway. ''I'll send someone over shortly to take your statement.''

''I won't be going anywhere until tomorrow, unless I'm in your way.''

''Not in ours.'' Wilkie stepped out of the trailer and waited for Copps to follow. Copps closed the door behind him and the two men crossed the clearing to join the little group on the porch of the cabin.

''Nice tits,'' Copps said. ''Pretty hair, too. She should grow it out.''

''ONE BLOW, administered from behind, with something like a baseball bat, but not heavy enough to kill him,'' the medical examiner was saying. ''A second wound is more serious, on the side of his head, but it may have been caused by falling against the stove. The corner of the stove fits the wound. I would say he died eight to twelve hours ago.''

Wilkie grunted and turned to the technician. ''You finished?''

''Unless you want me to look for something special.''

Wilkie shook his head. ''We'll send him to the lab, see if they can find anybody else's hairs on him.'' He nodded to the ambulance men to take the body away. To the two policemen who had been first on the scene, he said, ''Tape the place off until we've turned it over thoroughly. You can open up the road, but keep this gate blocked.'' To Copps, he said, ''Get a formal statement from the girl before we go.''

''What's her name again?'' Copps asked.

''Eliza Pollock. Wait, run me into town first, then come back and get the statement, and pick me up when you've got it.''

''Where? Where will you be?''

''In that diner by Harlan's motel. The one Pickett's wife used to run.''

FOUR

In Greenbank, they stopped at the Chicken Coop and bought four loaves of whole wheat, which, frozen, would last them two weeks, ate a breakfast of cinnamon buns and coffee, and drove on to Lindsay, where they bought those groceries unavailable in the IGA store in Larch River. They continued north.

As they approached Larch River, Charlotte said, "I told Harlan I'd fill in for him at the diner while we're up here if he wants. Rose quit on him two weeks ago and he's had to use high-school kids until he gets a proper replacement. I'll get to say hello to everybody. Let's just put the groceries away and go over there, see how he's fixed. Then you want to go up to the cabin, right?"

"I'd like to see how it got through the winter. See how that tenant is treating it."

"And see Eliza."

"And see Eliza."

They pulled up in front of Charlotte's house, waved to a neighbor, called across to another, and let themselves in. All the doors and windows were secure and the furnace was functioning, so they turned the heat up a few degrees, switched on the fridge, unloaded the groceries, then drove over to Harlan's diner.

SERGEANT WILKIE was drinking coffee at the counter, just as if he was waiting for them. He shook hands with Pickett and said, "First chance I've had to congratulate you two. But then, I didn't get an invitation to the wedding." Pickett said, "Nobody did. But thanks." He sat down next to Wilkie, and Charlotte smiled, touched Wilkie on the shoulder, and went behind the unattended counter, poured them each a cup of coffee, then disappeared through a door at the end of the room to look for her former boss.

Finally, into this odd silence, Pickett asked, "So? What are you doing here?"

"It's our territory now, ever since Lyman Caxton went."

Larch River had had one of the last one-man police forces in Ontario; then the police chief, Lyman Caxton, had handed in his badge when his girlfriend's brother was discovered to be a killer and she left town.

"I know that. I didn't know that an OPP officer with your seniority—staff sergeant, is it?—still had to get his hands dirty. What happened?"

"You haven't heard?" Wilkie looked at him over his coffee mug.

"Heard what?"

"Sorry. I was waiting for you to say something. We've got a probable homicide. I was just about to call you."

"I'm retired, didn't you know? You'll have to manage on your own."

"Somebody killed your tenant last night. Norbert Thompson. Hit him with a baseball bat, though he might've been killed by the stove as he fell."

Charlotte reappeared to stand beside Pickett. She had obviously heard the news already. "Harlan just told me," she said. "You know anything else?"

"We don't know who did it. He was found dead about two hours ago."

"Who found him?" Pickett asked.

"Girl who lives in your trailer."

"Oh, Jesus. Eliza. Was the guy a mess? We'd better get up there, see how she is. Put your coat on, Charlotte."

"Harlan just asked me if I'd take over right away. He's been tending the counter himself."

"In an hour, tell him. Let's go up to see Eliza first." He turned to Wilkie. "Is she still in the trailer?"

"That's where I left her. But tell me about this guy Thompson before you run away."

"I don't know much. I let it be known that I wouldn't mind having a tenant in the cabin, not for the rent but just to kind of caretake it until we came back. You know, some kid throws a rock through the window and then another one, and the place is derelict before the winter's over. There isn't much to stop anyone from turning the place over."

Wilkie said, "If you're talking about us, then there never was. We can't drive up and down every country road twenty-four hours a day, protecting uninhabited summer places of rich city folk, can we?"

"Were we better off with Lyman Caxton as the town cop?"

"Probably, as long as he had us for backup. But that was then, this is now. They couldn't find a replacement for Lyman for the wages they paid, so they contracted with us.'' Wilkie drank some coffee. "We've had a series of break-ins around here lately. Serious burglaries. I think it's locals, myself. Did you know this township has the highest break-in rate in the county?''

"I lost some stuff when I was building the cabin. Lyman got my chain saw back when he turned over Siggy Siggurdson's place looking for the gun that killed Timmy Marlow, so we thought.''

"The only thing we've got to go on is that all the break-ins have happened on Friday nights.''

"Kids. The kind that break into summer cottages along the river.''

"Maybe. But beating a guy's head in? Old guy? Is *that* kids?''

"There are different kinds of kids. But he was younger than me and he wasn't helpless. He'd worked on a farm all his life. I think he was about as fragile as I am. Maybe there are two gangs.''

Wilkie looked at him sharply. "What are you talking about?''

"You just said it could be locals or it could be professionals, a gang from Newcastle. It could be both. I mean, if word gets out that there's a gang working the whole area on Friday nights, then somebody around here might think that's a bright idea. Somebody stupid.''

"Where did he come from, your tenant?''

"From the country. Not far away. That right, Charlotte?''

She pulled a stool out from under the counter and sat down opposite them. "He used to run a chicken farm for the Maguires, up past the lake. The farm supplied most of the eggs and chickens around here for people who didn't have their own. The Maguires used to manage it themselves, the two of them. Then Maguire got sick, one of those diseases that go on for years, and he sent for his brother Norbert to help out. Norbert was working as a janitor in a school in New Brunswick, but he'd been raised on a farm and done that kind of work most of his life. Anyway, he came here about three years ago and did everything, including helping out with nursing the brother. People said that without Norbert, she'd have had to hire two other people.''

Charlotte looked around the diner, which was now filling up with curious customers, people who had seen the OPP car outside and heard the news. Even without Wilkie's car parked there, indicating that something was happening, the coffee shop was where the town picked up its gossip.

Wilkie asked, ''How come these brothers had different names?''

Charlotte lowered her voice. ''It's to do with the way the family was broken up when they were kids. Ask Mrs. Sproat—Mrs. Maguire, she was. Let me get on with the story. What happened was that Maguire died last November, I think it was. Everyone expected Norbert to take his place. It would have been natural enough. Instead of that, she went into Sweetwater one day and came back with a new husband, and I guess told Norbert he wouldn't be needed anymore. Anyway, Norbert left the farm and got a room in town. He used to eat here in the diner sometimes. He found some odd jobs to do, working on a Christmas-tree farm first, a bit of fencing, stuff like that, so when

Mel was looking for a tenant for the cabin, I suggested Norbert because he would know how to keep it up, and Mel offered him the place for free for three months, at least until we came back. I felt sorry for the guy, and besides, it's a bit isolated, and Eliza—have you met her? Eliza Pollock?—yes, she wanted to use the trailer on weekends, and we felt better knowing that someone was within call.''

"You *have* talked to Eliza?" Pickett asked Wilkie.

"I'm getting a statement. She didn't see anything."

"Good. Let's go, Charlotte. Eliza might need something."

Wilkie looked at his watch. "Will you stay up there until noon?"

"Right. You're not done. Sorry. Sure. We'll wait for you in the cabin or the trailer."

"In the trailer. The cabin's still out of bounds."

IN THE CAR, Charlotte asked, "What does he mean?"

"He means they haven't finished blowing fingerprint powder over everything, or whatever the equivalent is around here—sawdust maybe. We'll let them get on with it. Just see how Eliza is."

"Maybe she'll be too shook up to want to stay."

"That's what I wondered. But she's pretty tough."

"I'm not. I'd like her out of there until someone's living in the cabin."

"I should tell her to find somewhere else to sleep?"

"She can come stay with us if she likes. I just don't want her by herself down there. And Mel, dear, don't tell me to get my coat on just when I've agreed to stay to help Harlan out. Or at any time. Ask me, okay?''

"I wasn't telling you, just saying we'd better get going.''

"You weren't asking me, though, were you?''

"Sorry.''

"No, you're not, except for upsetting me in some way. Think about it.''

ELIZA WAS JUST AS dismissive of their concern for her safety as Pickett was of Eliza's having any say in the matter of whether she should move into town and stay with them.

"Get your things together," he said as soon as they were inside the trailer. "The stuff in the fridge will be okay." He started to move around the trailer, making small tidying-up gestures to help her get ready for their departure.

She watched him for a while, about fifteen seconds, then asked, "What's the matter? Somebody paint a red cross on the door? 'Here Be Plague'?''

Pickett stopped folding chairs and stacking them on the bunk. "You can't stay here, can you?''

"Are they going to cut the power off? The town hauling the trailer away for back taxes?''

"What are you talking about?''

Charlotte said, "It's my fault, Eliza. I said I don't think you're safe here. I think you should come with us for the weekend." She added, "We have plenty of room.''

Eliza moved quickly around the table and stayed Pickett's hand as he started to open the door to the bedroom. "I'll be all right.''

Pickett said, "Someone could break in here with a rolled-up newspaper."

"Someone would get a surprise."

"You? What could you do against a guy with a baseball bat?"

"Don't *worry* about it. Okay, Mel? Charlotte, tell him not to worry about me."

Charlotte slowed down, glanced around the room and moved away from them to the end of the trailer, as if to leave them to sort it out. "You mean don't nag, right?" She smiled. "You'd better tell him, Eliza."

"Tell him what?"

"Why you aren't worried about being attacked." She smiled again and looked away.

Eliza turned to Pickett. "Because I won't be by myself. Here. Tonight."

"What do you mean?"

Charlotte said, "She means there will be someone else here, too. I *think* that's what 'won't be alone' means. Am I right, honey?"

Pickett said, "You mean you've got someone coming?"

Charlotte burst out laughing, and Eliza, though embarrassed, giggled along with her.

Pickett, totally confused, said, "Why didn't you say so?"

"At what point? To whom?" Eliza asked.

Charlotte said, "Come on, Mel." To Eliza, she said, "Come up to the house for supper anyway, both of you. No? Good. The chicken's too small. Otherwise, you'd be welcome."

"Can I bring him for breakfast tomorrow?"

"We get up too early for that. No, make it some other weekend. Come on, Mel."

Outside, Pickett asked, "Why didn't you let her come for breakfast?"

"Because she didn't mean it. She was just saying she would like to, other things being equal, and she also wanted to say 'he' or, rather, 'him' out loud."

"Huh?"

"For Heaven's sake, she wanted to be sure you heard right. She spends her weekends up here with a boyfriend."

"I thought she came up here to write a book. How did you know, by the way?"

"The bedroom door was shut, and she was making sure you didn't get past her to open it."

FIVE

SERGEANT WILKIE HAD been born and raised in Toronto, and he joined the Ontario Provincial Police after a spell in the Toronto force because his idea of small-town life, derived from sentimental accounts of rural childhoods he had seen on television, had led him to believe that the simple world of the small town had to be preferable to the gritty squalor he coped with on the night shift in Toronto's Fifty-third Division. He had not found it to be so.

It was true that most of Sweetwater's violence was domestic, but he soon forgot the jungle he had left and began to miss the city. He missed the anonymity when he was off duty; half the population of Sweetwater knew him by sight, so that to take a day off, to have a meal out, like a civilian, he had to drive to Lindsay. Even there, he bumped into people who knew him from Sweetwater, so to be really anonymous, he had to go back to his starting point, Toronto.

And in Sweetwater, he was always being reminded that he was an outsider. Everybody else, including most of his colleagues, knew things, country things, that he didn't. They could tell at a glance when a woodstove was burning too hot, when a dog was rabid, how to cook venison, how much one of the local wooden houses was worth, stuff like that. And they would know, driving out toward Donnington to the place where Norbert Thompson used to live, what a chicken farm looked like, while Wilkie, certain he was wrong, nevertheless kept his eyes open for several acres of fluffy yellow chicks pecking corn that had been distributed from a giantess's apron.

What he found seemed to him to be a miniature concentration camp: a gate in a chain-link fence around rows of low metal buildings, without a human in sight. The road through the farm led past these buildings to the original farmhouse, made of brick with freshly painted trim, surrounded by well-kept grass, and at the back, a vegetable patch. And just beyond the farmhouse stood a fine old barn, now a garage and storage building, in nearly as good condition as it had been a hundred years before. These two buildings, the house and the barn, had an antique, preserved air in contrast to the chicken sheds, which were sided with aluminum.

Wilkie pulled up in front of the house, and two dogs appeared from the barn, barking hard. One of the things Wilkie could not yet do was to recognize when a farm dog was trained to tear the throat out of a stranger and when it was just saying hello, so he stayed where he was. The door of the house opened and a woman appeared. Wilkie opened his car door an inch and waited while she called to the dogs, who moved back a foot, just enough to allow him to get down.

"Come on up," she said. "They won't bother you while I'm here."

Wilkie crossed the yard and climbed the steps to the porch, avoiding any sudden movement. The dogs stayed with him all the way, an inch away from his calves, then turned and took off after another perceived intruder across the field. The woman led him inside and pointed to a chair, taking one herself.

Very little had been done to bring the house into the last half of the twentieth century. Wilkie noted that most of the furnishings dated from before his time, although they looked merely old rather than antique. A rail-backed bench with a padded seat filled the space along one wall. Wilkie and Mrs. Sproat sat opposite each other in wooden armchairs with thin corduroy pads on the seats; three straight-backed chairs were positioned, one on each wall, ready to be brought into service when company called. A braided rug filled the center of the floor, which was made of wide planking rubbed to a high polish.

There were no side tables of any kind. All of the chairs were within reach of the only raised surface in the room: a large pine table on stubby, two-foot legs, obviously cut down from its original dining height. On this, a bunch of bulrushes made the only purely decorative object in the room, except for some views of Scotland on the walls, framed like religious texts in quarter-inch pine trim that crossed at the corners.

They had entered the house through the kitchen. Wilkie surmised that the front door and the room they were sitting in were used only for funerals and festivities. A huge yellow refrigerator dominated the kitchen they had passed through, but everything else in the room looked like pioneer equipment, made of chipped enamel, scrubbed pine, and iron. Wilkie assumed at first sight that he was in a typical Ontario farmhouse, but as the detail of his surroundings pressed itself on him, he realized that the few farm-houses he had been inside were nothing like this, that farmers today knew about dishwashers and freezers and microwaves, and that most of them had replaced the old heavy wooden storm windows with aluminum.

Here, he was sitting in a time warp, a museum, and once he had found that word, it made sense of everything he saw, because the place was perfectly maintained. The fences, the paintwork on the buildings, the gravel road, and the grassed areas were all closely attended to. The house inside smelled of laundry soap and of wax, though underneath there was a mild Granny's-apron smell of ancient fabric, as though the air was not changed often enough.

"Nice place," Wilkie said, taking out his notebook and a pencil.

"My great-great-grandfather built it. He came out from Scotland in eighteen eighty-seven with enough money to build this house and, later on, six farm buildings. Only the barn and house are left. It was a mixed farm then; my grandfather moved it over to chickens. Now, what do you want?" She pulled her cardigan around her shoulders and sniffled, shivering. The tour was now complete, she was saying.

Wilkie said, "I can come back."

"You do what you have to do, then maybe I can get some peace."

"Norbert Thompson," Wilkie said, playing with the notebook. "I'm sorry to tell you—"

"That he's dead," she interrupted. "I heard about it this morning. Three people came by to tell me. Different times."

"You heard how it happened?"

"Somebody hit him last night, they say."

Wilkie nodded.

"Strangers?" She sniffled hard.

"We don't know. I can come back tomorrow," he repeated as she sniffled again.

"If you think I'm upset, I'm not; it's because I've got a bad cold. I'm sorry Norbert's dead, of course. I'll pray for him, and I'll pay for his funeral if he didn't leave enough, but I wasn't that close to him, so I can't grieve a lot."

"He did work here, though?"

"He did. For about four years. But that don't make him close. He was a necessity, and a servant, if you like, not a friend. We had respect for each other, though."

"What did he do here?"

"Everything I couldn't. He was the hired man."

Wilkie thought, my first "hired man." "Why did he leave?" he asked.

"Because we didn't need him anymore."

"You let him go?"

"He wanted to go. My husband thought it was best."

"Maybe I should be talking to your husband." Wilkie looked around the room with a where-is-he? air.

"He's in Lindsay, selling the eggs. It doesn't matter. This is *my* farm. Norbert Thompson was *my* hired man. Wives should submit to their husbands, but Norbert Thompson goes back to before Mr. Sproat was here. So I'll answer for those days."

"How was it you didn't need him anymore? Did you close down some part of the operation?"

"I got married again, to Mr. Sproat, and I, that is we, my husband and I, didn't need Norbert anymore. Norbert could see that himself, but he waited until Aaron raised the matter."

"Aaron?"

"Mr. Sproat. My husband. Norbert needed to know that he should give up his job."

Wilkie began to feel a stubbornness in her. He was not sure if he should trust his feelings, though. Maybe disgorging tiny pieces of information instead of telling the whole story at once was typical of country ways. If so, he could wait.

"When did you and Mr. Sproat get married?"

"Just before Christmas."

"Was Thompson surprised?"

"Oh, he was surprised all right. It was none of his business, of course, but I can see that some surprise would be natural from his point of view."

"He did live here?"

"He did. In the back room. Downstairs."

"Did you cook for him?"

"Of course I did. He was the hired man."

"You said he was here for four years. What did you do before he came?"

"He didn't come until we finally needed him. Before that, Mr. Maguire, my first husband, did all the work."

While he waited for her to expand her response, Wilkie tried to guess her age and character. Somewhere between forty and seventy was as close as he could come. Her slightly weathered look—the local equivalent of a Florida tan—made it hard to guess any closer. She wore no lipstick or any other makeup, and her hair, grayish-brown, was netted up in a kind of snood. She wore the sort of dress meant to be worked in, coarse brown stockings, and carpet slippers. Two gold rings, one on the third finger of each hand, were her only ornaments. Wilkie wondered what kind of wife she was—the house was spotless, but there was no lingering smell of cooking.

"So, there was a time when you and your first husband lived here with Norbert Thompson, the hired man. Why did you start four years ago to need a hired man?" He had not forgotten what Charlotte had said about Maguire's illness, but he was trying to find the right note to strike.

"Because my first husband got cancer. I needed Norbert to do the chores and help me, in looking after Mr. Maguire."

"Who?"

"My first husband."

"Ah. Right. So Norbert Thompson ran the farm while your husband was sick, and then your husband died, but your second husband didn't need Thompson's help."

She said nothing.

"Where did you find Thompson?"

"Mr. Maguire sent for him."

"Sent to where?"

"To the family he lived with in New Brunswick."

Was that a glint in her eye? Was she enjoying fucking around like this? "What was the connection between your first husband and Norbert Thompson that your husband could just send for him?"

"They was brothers. Didn't I say?"

"No. But Maguire? Thompson? Who changed his name?"

"Mr. Maguire came from a big family. When his mother died, the children was split up among whoever would take them in. Mr. Maguire's brother, Norbert, got adopted by a couple down in New Brunswick name of Thompson, who had his name changed. But he always knew who he was really, and the couple did right by making sure he knew where the rest of his family was. We got and sent a Christmas card every year. He made a trip once to see us, about ten years ago."

"When did your husband die? What month?"

"October, it was."

"And you were married again by Christmas?"

"December fifteen. Our minister said there was no need to wait."

"Were you all three here for Christmas?"

"Yes. Norbert left after New Year's. I paid him an extra month's wages."

"Tell me about him. What kind of a man was he? Did he drink?"

"Saturday afternoons he used to go in to Sweet-water, to do some errands for the farm and take his laundry to the Laundromat there. I looked after the sheets and stuff, but he did his own laundry, and I don't have a machine. Afterward, he would spend time in the beer parlor. He was never what they call drunk—I wouldn't allow that, I'm Gospel—but you could smell it on him. The minister said it wasn't my affair so long as he didn't bring it in the house, which he didn't."

"Did he have any friends?"

"In the beer parlor, p'raps. None came to the house."

"What about enemies?"

"Where would he make enemies? He was from New Brunswick. He didn't know anyone around here except the people we dealt with, and the mailman. Whoever did for him was a stranger, I reckon, one of those breaking into houses. That's what they say."

"Did he have any money, do you know?"

She took her time to respond. "He could have saved quite a bit over the time he was here. And he might have brought some with him from New Brunswick. He got his board and room free, and he never bought anything. Mr. Maguire was bedridden when he came, so Norbert gradually wore out all his clothes which I gave him. I believe he might have had a fair bit."

Wilkie nodded, making a note to search the cabin properly for Thompson's stash.

"What's your second husband's name, again, Mrs. Sproat? His first name?"

"Aaron."

"Aaron Sproat. What was his trade?"

"He drove the truck for the feed supplier."

"That how you met him?"

"No. He didn't supply us. I met him in church. We belonged to the same congregation, the First Gospel Church on River Street. Mr. Maguire's family was one of those that broke away when the Evangelicals split, and the Gospel congregation was formed. I switched over when the Evangelicals started to hold services with other congregations. Mixed faith is no faith, to my way of thinking. If you believe in something, you believe in it and everyone else is wrong. Isn't that sense? I don't hold with persecution—I think we should be tolerant while they are in error, let God punish them—but you have to believe your way is right. And once you figure out what's true and what isn't, and what the Lord wants from you, then everything you need is in the Book.''

"Was Norbert Thompson a member of your church?''

"Norbert didn't have no religion. At least he never spoke of any to me. I never pursued it with him. We do hold with conversion, but after being cooped up with him all week, I didn't want to spend my Sundays with him, too.''

"So he never met Mr. Sproat until after your husband died?''

"That's correct.''

"Did he know about him?''

"Know what, mister? Know what? There was nothing to know. I had a husband living. Mr. Sproat respected that. We strictly passed the time of day after church, until Mr. Maguire died. I used to stay over for an hour, and pretty soon Mr. Sproat and I understood each other. We got to know each other pretty good after three or four years. He was a good friend during that time, and he's been a worthy husband since. So then I was free and so was he.''

"And he would know about chicken farming, of course.''

"He's a strong man, a bit past his prime, but he's lifted sacks of feed all his life, so he doesn't find this work heavy.''

"Did you stay friendly with Thompson when he moved out?"

"I was civil. He was the hired man, just. My husband's brother, true, but we never was friends, no. He didn't live enough in the Lord's way for me, though he respected my ways in the house. And he did the work all right. But he wasn't in the right state."

Two beers a week and you're doomed, thought Wilkie. No—damned. "Did he never come back for a visit?"

"A couple of times to sort out some things. He didn't have any transportation. Not that it would be that far to walk, but he wasn't interested in us, or us in him. Not to socialize."

Wilkie wondered how Thompson had amused himself in the house. "Could I have a glass of water?" he asked, meaning tea or coffee, hoping to find a way to get her to chat a little further.

"Are we finished?"

"For the moment. I'll need to talk to your husband."

"He'll be back around suppertime. But he'll have a lot of work to do when he gets in."

"I'll come back tomorrow."

"Make it in the afternoon. I suppose all days are the same in your work, but tomorrow's Sunday." She stood up and walked out to the kitchen.

Wilkie heard the tap run, and then she called to him, "Here's your water." She was standing by the kitchen door, holding a jelly glass of water. Wilkie drank half of it and handed the glass back. It was good water but too cold, and he had never much liked the stuff.

She opened the door and stood back to let him out, closing it on his heels.

SIX

"HE CAME TO Charlotte to see if he could put up a notice in the coffee shop inquiring if anyone had a room for rent. He was also looking for work. Harlan, who owns the coffee shop, and the gas pump, and the motel, and most of the rest of Larch River, took him on, at below the minimum of course, to give the motel a coat of paint and to do some maintenance work. I think what Harlan paid him just about covered his groceries, and Charlotte felt sorry for him—he seemed like a bit of an innocent for a man his age—and she suggested to me that I might let him have the cabin free until the spring. I didn't know anything about the guy except that he was out of a job and had no place to stay, but I drove out toward Donnington to see the farm and I figured anyone who has run a chicken farm and kept up a farmhouse the way he had was a good bet for a tenant. So I said yes, and he moved in."

They were sitting in the cabin, drinking coffee. Sergeant Wilkie had appeared just as they were leaving, and Pickett had stayed to talk with him. Charlotte had gone back to her house. It was late on Saturday afternoon. The police had finished scouring and recording the scene of the crime, the body had been removed, and the stove lit.

"Did you meet him very often?" Wilkie asked.

"Just once. When I agreed he could come, Charlotte took over and moved the guy in. He didn't have a car or anything. He had to walk back and forth to town, to work."

"Was he still working for Harlan?"

"No. He got everything of Harlan's painted and fixed up. Then he started to do little jobs around the town, mainly ones he got through the hardware store—you know, repairing windows for widows, stuff like that. There's not as much call for handymen here as in Toronto, but I guess just enough to keep Thompson eating."

"Did your friend in the trailer report having many visitors?"

"You'll have to ask her."

"No carloads of kids? No punks?"

"No, she's only come up two or three times in the winter. Once she couldn't turn in at the lane because of the snow. Thompson had dug a footpath, but it hadn't been plowed yet. Eliza started coming regularly the last two or three weekends."

"I'll talk to her again. Come on. I'll take you home. I'll get you to come back later."

AT CHARLOTTE'S HOUSE, where they lived now when they were in Larch River, she tried to persuade Wilkie to stay for supper, but he declined, giving the impression that his wife was making an elaborate dinner that she wanted him to be on time for. In fact, on this night he would have a choice between frozen lasagna or chili, also frozen, because he did not want to be seen too often in one of the town's restaurants. He felt sorry for himself and didn't want anyone else to feel sorry for him, too.

Wilkie's wife Helen was an academic administrator. When they married, she had been a clerk in a dean's office at York University in Toronto, and he had been a constable with the Metropolitan Toronto Police Force. She liked her work; she liked the university; she liked Toronto, even the badlands where the university was located. She claimed still to love Wilkie, but he was beginning not to believe her. They might have fared better if he had stayed with the Metro police, but he had grown to dislike patrolling downtown Toronto—he had joined the force only because his father had been a policeman, and lately jobs had become hard to find—and believing his glumness was caused by the city, he had resigned and joined the provincial force, to work in the country.

"What about me?" Helen had asked. "Do I get consulted? Am I supposed to load up the wagon and follow you?"

"What else?"

"I've got a job of my own. And I like it."

That was the point when Wilkie realized that Helen's job meant more to her than a way of helping out with the groceries; she had created her own world. As his wife, she would have followed him to wherever he was posted. As herself, she would not. At first he had been posted to units in southern Ontario, close enough to enable her to commute to Toronto, but Sweetwater was two hours away, and four hours of driving on top of a day's work was too much, she found. So she had taken a room with her sister, who lived in midtown Toronto, where she stayed four nights a week, coming home on weekends, and at first, one night a week. Now she came home on Friday night and left at noon on Sunday to avoid the weekend traffic.

It was an arrangement that could only last until he was posted even farther away, but while it lasted, she did her best to make up for her absences. She cooked hard, leaving him with enough frozen meals to last the week, and they stayed in bed a lot during the two days she was there. But one day he would be posted to somewhere like Sioux Narrows, a thousand miles away in Northwest Ontario, and that would be that. Even Timmins, four hundred miles north, would be unmanageable. When that day came, they would have some hard decisions to make.

He was sure that in other circumstances, their marriage would have been as durable as most; but it was just a marriage, and so far, childless. In the end, her work would come first. Wilkie had wondered occasionally when she started to stay in the city if she had a boyfriend there, and he had tried the usual tricks—driving in unexpectedly, finding excuses to visit her at her sister's at odd hours, only to learn that she was entirely faithful.

His father had suggested that maybe she felt she was too good for him now that she had been promoted, but Helen was no snob, and she had no difficulty in being pleased with him at the occasional university function that would let her take him along. It was just, as she pointed out, that they had never discussed what being the wife of a provincial policeman was all about.

IN ANSWER TO Wilkie's next question, Charlotte described what little she knew about Thompson's life in New Brunswick. "He used to come in the restaurant sometimes for a cup of coffee. He told me it was a real treat, because the Maguires did not drink coffee, only herb tea."

"Was this part of their religion?"

"Probably. I heard there wasn't any church around here strict enough for them. Norbert never went with them to church, but he had to toe the line in the house, so he never got any coffee at home."

"Why did he stay?"

Charlotte tried for an answer. "Maybe he felt needed. Wanted, too. Maybe it was a home. He used to sort of brag about his brother like a kid, as if he was proud just of *having* a brother. You'd have to look at how he was raised after his mother died."

"And yet they pretty well kicked him out, right?"

"His sister-in-law and her new husband did, yes. After his brother died. At least, that's how it looked. Norbert never said anything about it while I was listening."

Wilkie said, "In a way, it would have made more sense if Thompson had killed Sproat, not got killed himself, wouldn't it?"

"In a way."

"Can you come back up to the cabin tomorrow, Mel? I'd like you to take a good look around. See if anything catches your eye."

"Nothing caught my eye so far, but okay."

"Pick you up here about ten."

PICKETT HAD ERECTED his cabin on a rise of land in the middle of five acres of otherwise undeveloped bush. On the edge of the lot, separated from the cabin by a patch of dense scrub, a small pond, fed by an underground stream, supported a pair of otters. The pond should have been the redeeming feature of the site, but Pickett had not yet cut a proper trail to it from the clearing. The cabin sat on a naturally bare patch of land where an ancient glacier had thrust up a mound of rock so smooth it had never acquired topsoil. Outside this area, Pickett had cut back the bush to make sufficient grounds for the trailer and two storage sheds he had built.

A trail wide enough for a one-ton truck led from the road up to the clearing. Beyond the fence, the trail met Duck Lake Road, the graveled county road that ran from Larch River, a mile away, to the bridge over the river, where it split east and west to serve the summer community along the riverbank.

When Pickett bought the lot, it was untouched; the timber was too scrubby to be worth harvesting, even for pulpwood, and there was nothing obviously pretty about the site to attract anyone wanting to build a summer cottage. Most of all, the rock, swamp, and pond created too many obstacles to any conventional development, and there was no access to water suitable for swimming or fishing. But Pickett had only been looking for an outdoor workshop, a piece of land on which he could try building a log cabin just for the experience, and the place suited him perfectly.

Although some of the locals had let him know afterward that he had been grossly overcharged, he didn't mind because it was still a cheap piece of land by city or lakefront standards, and he had built his cabin on the rock, liked what he had done, and decided to live there when the weather permitted, tinkering with such landscaping as the site allowed. Then he had met Charlotte and they had begun the pleasant process of deciding how best to enjoy all their properties.

WILKIE PARKED in the road and they ducked under the tape that was keeping sightseers away, for the townspeople were still driving by to look at the scene of the crime, stopping for the ritual five minutes in case there was anything of interest to see. The two men walked to the trailer, where Pickett called Eliza, hoping to get a look at her mysterious boyfriend, but whoever he was, he stayed out of sight. They came back along the path and followed the yellow tape to the cabin.

"We've done the house and these paths," Wilkie said. "I'm hoping we don't have to do the rest." He waved a hand at the thick tangle of brush around the cabin.

"There's just one path I cut through, to see where the property line runs. It starts behind the cabin and goes to the line—nowhere, really, but it might seem promising to someone trying to find another way out, so I'd take a look along that."

Wilkie nodded. "We've already done it. My boys couldn't figure out why it stopped. So we'll go over the clearing and the paths again and take a look along the edges. If we have to go into the brush, I'll get more men."

Pickett asked, "You looking for anything special?"

"The usual. A baseball bat with blood on it. The killer's wallet with his picture in it. You know."

They entered the cabin and Wilkie moved to the telephone to organize his team. Before he spoke, he fumbled an envelope from his jacket pocket and gave it to Pickett, who was standing in the doorway surveying the cabin.

Pickett took out the picture of the dead man lying as Eliza had found him, facedown on the floor. He studied the photograph for a long time, then put it on the seat of a chair and began to look around. His job was to find something missing or out of place. It was a small chance, because any discrepancy between his memory and what he saw could probably be accounted for by the fact that Thompson had been living there for three months. The man was entitled to rearrange the furniture and ornaments to suit himself, and also to break or lose something without scrupulously reporting it to Pickett. But Pickett was a policeman, and Wilkie thought it was worth a try.

He began in the bedroom. A few work clothes, a laundry bag, an extra belt, and a red-flannel nightcap with a tassel—unused, and almost certainly some kind of joke gift or prize—hung from the row of hooks Pickett had put up to serve as a closet. On a single peg on the opposite wall, an old black suit and a tie were draped on a wire hanger, and a pair of polished black shoes was lined up on the floor, the whole ensemble reminiscent of whatever formal occasions Thompson had been called upon to attend in the last thirty years. A small pine bureau, which Pickett had bought from an antiques store because it seemed to be the kind of thing a pioneer might have made, contained a few pairs of socks, some underwear, and three shirts neatly ironed and folded, but without the starch of a laundry finish.

Pickett came out of the bedroom, looked around the kitchen—none of the implements was missing—the little bathroom, and then less attentively around the main room; which had been thoroughly scoured by Wilkie's men.

"I can't see anything unusual," he said to Wilkie.

"Outside?"

Outside, stove wood was stacked on the deck of the porch, as always. The main woodpile had collapsed slightly, but no more than it would have from natural depletion. There was nothing else.

"So he opened the door to a caller, turned around, and got clobbered."

"What with?" Pickett asked.

"Something heavy, round, and smooth."

Pickett said, "He was hit with a piece of two-inch oak dowelling, about two feet long."

Wilkie grinned. "Now just tell me the color of the villain's eyes, his height, which leg he limped on, and I'll have him picked up this afternoon."

But Pickett was looking at the photograph again. "He could've been waiting. Inside."

"Who, for Chrissake? What are you talking about?"

Pickett stared at him for a while, then broke out of his thoughts. "Sorry. Sorry. Look, I'll show you. Gimme a hand." He moved to the end of the couch and signaled for Wilkie to go to the other end. The couch was made of pine, the back and seat identical so that it could be converted into a double bed by lowering the back.

"Lift it up," Pickett said. Wilkie raised his end off the floor. "No," Pickett said. "Like this." He pressed the back of the couch down toward the seat and took out the peg that held the back in place. Wilkie, watching, did the same at his end, and they lowered the couch flat onto the floor: a bed.

Pickett held up his peg, a piece of dowelling about three inches long. "This couch was the first thing I bought to sleep on. Then I moved it in here when I got the bed. It was missing one of these pegs at first, so I got a piece of two-inch dowelling and made a new one. Now I had two feet of two-inch, finished-oak dowelling I didn't need. I chucked it in the wood box, but I could never bring myself to burn it—it costs about a dollar an inch, and besides, it was a nice piece of oak. So I left it there in case I ever had a need for it. It's not there now."

"So Thompson burned it."

Pickett shook his head. "Maybe. I doubt it, though. He noticed it when I was showing him around, admired it, because he was a bit of a carpenter himself. I told him how I had come by it, and he agreed it was too good to burn. In fact, he got it out of the box and stood it against the wall so it wouldn't get burned by mistake."

"It was always simple when Sherlock explained it, too."

"Huh?"

"Nothing. So he let the guy in, then got clobbered?"

"Could be."

"Or he opened the door, warylike, with the wood in his hand, and the guy took it off him and clobbered him? No. Thompson was hit from behind."

"So?"

"So nothing. You could make up ten stories to fit. There was no sign of a fight, or even of a scuffle."

"Then either he knew the caller or someone was waiting for him in the cabin."

"Either way, we're looking for a piece of oak dowelling. Right? You watch a lot of TV?" Wilkie pointed at the set on the table.

"That's Thompson's. I did without."

"Really? I'd've taken you for an addict of those Sunday-night shows."

There was a knock on the door. Eliza stood on the porch with a tray. "I figured you guys might like a cup of coffee, so I made enough for everybody. Do I still have to walk down to the road and come back up the path to get over here?" She pointed behind her to the yellow tape that marked out the permitted walkways.

"Just for another hour or so," Wilkie said. "We'll sweep the yard now. The team is on its way back."

She watched him pour out two cups of coffee and then look inquiringly at her. She shook her head. "I'll have mine in the trailer."

AN HOUR LATER, Pickett said to Charlotte, "The only thing I could tell you about the guy is that he was clean."

"Clean?"

"Yeah. I guess I was kind of braced for a bunkhouse scene—you know, a fifty-year-old bachelor living alone, maybe a one-man mining camp. I just assumed he would have lived a little rough, but all the stuff in the drawers was clean, and he had this bag hanging on the wall with the week's—I guess it was a week's—dirty stuff. Nothing smelled at all. Even the bed looked as if he changed the sheets every week. But I didn't see anything else that showed what kind of person he was. None of his own reading matter—magazines, books, not even a newspaper. Just this television set that he'd put on the table in the middle of the room."

"What did he cook for himself?"

"There wasn't much there—bacon and eggs, couple of tins of stew, cold cuts, bread and jam. Didn't look as if he'd ever learned."

SEVEN

THE NEXT AFTERNOON, Wilkie gave Pickett back his cabin. Everything had been measured, photographed, and dusted, and the yard and the first few feet of brush around the cabin had been scoured in the search for a two-foot piece of dowelling. While Pickett tidied up the remaining few traces of Thompson's tenure, Charlotte scrubbed off the black, greasy photographic powder that seemed to be everywhere.

When Pickett could find nothing else to do, he said, "Let's invite Eliza and her boyfriend to supper."

"Tonight? Here? For canned stew? There aren't even any crackers."

"No. Up to the house. Pizza. That's what they were probably planning to have anyway. The Pizza Palace next to the gas station just opened for the summer. We'll pick some up on the way home."

"Do we have any wine? Did he look more of a wine or a beer person?"

"I'd say beer. He was drooling a bit and scratching his balls. Actually, I haven't seen him yet. Hang on." He disappeared and came back ten minutes later. "Still didn't see him, but Eliza said she'd bring some wine."

"What time?"

"Five." Pickett looked at his watch. "They're driving back to Toronto tonight."

Charlotte untied her apron. "We'd better scram. Get some ice cream at the IGA."

ELIZA'S BOYFRIEND WAS a surprise. Pickett had first met Eliza two years before when they had both been involved in the production of a Canadian version of *She Stoops to Conquer*. And then, on a golden day in the fall, Eliza and her then boyfriend went for a hike in the bush, paused in a little grove blanketed and cushioned with pine needles, to discover when they returned to the trail that they had been making love twenty feet from a body lodged in a crevice in the rock. They had come for help to Pickett's cabin, the nearest house.

The discovery had revealed a deficiency in the boyfriend, a lack of the instincts the circumstances called for. The lovers had become estranged as a result and she left him, but by then, Eliza was vital to the theater group and she now needed somewhere to stay until the play was ready, so Pickett had offered her the little house trailer he had used while building the cabin. Since then, she had used it as a kind of weekend cottage on the understanding that her job was to keep the trailer, and the cabin when it wasn't occupied, from looking derelict simply by keeping the weeds— young spruce trees, most of them—out of the path. It was also understood that Pickett might sell the trailer at any time, since of all his dwellings, it was certainly the one most obviously surplus to his requirements, but once Eliza was installed, he made no effort to do so.

She stood in the doorway now, in one hand carrying a bottle of wine, and with her other hand leading forward a coffee-colored stranger of medium height, dressed in a white shirt, blue jeans and sandals on bare feet. He smiled, waiting.

Pickett, not quite sure if he was to be introduced to this exotic—the man could just be asking for directions and Eliza holding on to him to prevent his native shyness from making him run away before he got them—wondered if someone would give him a signal.

The man put out his hand. "Sarwingupta," he said.

Pickett shook the hand and said nothing, waiting to find out what the sounds meant. The possibilities were several: "Sarwingupta"—the Sanskrit (?) equivalent of "Clarence"; "Sarwin, Gupta"—"Gupta" being the first name but offered last in accordance with polite Sikh practice; or just possibly "Sir Win Gupta", whose grandfather had been the last Indian to have a hereditary knighthood conferred on him before partition.

"Sarwin has been dying to meet you," Eliza said.

"Has he? Famous, am I? Then we'll have to arrange it. Come in, Sarwin. Come in. Sarwin, this is my wife, Charlotte. I'm Mel Pickett, by the way, Sarwin. No, no, you don't have to take your shoes off because of Eliza. She always does. It's not muddy, is it?" Pickett looked queryingly at Eliza. "Unless you'd feel more comfortable, of course." If your feet hurt, that is, or if that's the way you people always behave on a doorstep.

"The road *is* muddy," Eliza said, "and you've all got yours off." She kicked off her shoes and crossed the threshold. "Come on, Gupta." Gupta followed suit.

"Beer, Gupta?" Christ, no. Gupta was surely the man's *last* name; Eliza was just horsing around. "Or a scotch, Sarwin?"

"Beer, thanks, Mr. Pickett."

"Mel."

Gupta looked at Eliza. "Mel?" he asked.

"That's his name."

"Yes? An unusual name." He turned to Pickett. "Call me Sarwin. Like you did."

Eliza said to Charlotte, "You would never know they were both Canadian, would you? Sarwin was born in Edmonton. How about you, Mel?"

"Hamilton."

Charlotte said, "The pizza!" in tones that suggested it was filling the kitchen and now leaking out the windows. "I'll have some of your beer," she said to Pickett as she ran from the room.

"Give Sarwin a whiskey, Mel. He's been asking for it all weekend. It's his favorite forbidden drink. Wine for me," Eliza said.

"I asked for it *once,* last night, because you said you had some, then you couldn't find it. I haven't been asking for it repeatedly, for heaven's sake."

"Hold on, Sarwin. I've got some scotch here somewhere."

"I would rather have a beer. Really. Thank you. A beer."

"The scotch is around somewhere."

"A beer."

They might have gone on like this for some time, but they were interrupted by Willis, the dog, who came downstairs, took one look at Gupta and circled to attack. Pickett grabbed the dog and held her, yapping furiously, off the floor. "That's the first time she's ever taken after someone," he said.

"Dogs are very racist," Gupta said. "Babies, too. Very frightening I am to both kinds." He leaned forward and smiled at the dog. Willis recoiled in terror and barked an octave higher.

"Put her in the basement," Charlotte said.

"Does she bite?" Gupta asked.

"Not until you came along."

"Leave her, then. Better she should get used to me in case I come back. If she bites me, I'll kick her arse."

Pickett put Willis on the couch, where she dug herself in, still glaring at Gupta.

Charlotte brought in a pizza and a stack of plates and began cutting the pie into slices. "Sorry about this. Not much of a Sunday dinner, is it? But get Eliza to bring you to the house in Toronto and I'll cook you a proper Canadian Sunday dinner."

"Charlotte…" Eliza began.

"Yes, right. You were born in Edmonton. Sorry," Charlotte said to Gupta. "I keep thinking you're just off the boat." She smiled at him. "That's what they used to say after the war about those immigrants in long overcoats with belts tied all the way around. 'Just off the boat,' they used to say. Now you'd have to say 'just off the plane,' wouldn't you? Doesn't have the same ring, though, does it? Anyway, you're not. No. Have you two known each other long?"

"I edited a book Sarwin wrote."

"What's that mean? Corrected the spelling? The punctuation?"

"That's it. I corrected the spelling, and the grammar, things like that, didn't I, dear? Translated it practically, from the original pidgin."

"'Pidgin' is *African,* though its origin is Chinese, I think," Gupta told her.

Pickett asked, "What's the book about?"

"It's about why some immigrant groups retain their culture more and for a longer time than others."

"I see. What do you do for a living?"

"That's what I do. I'm a historian. Social history."

"Where do you work?"

"At Douglas University."

"And you teach about which immigrants keep their culture longest?"

"Ah, no. I teach the usual courses. European History to 1453, England 1815 to 1914, Canada before Confederation, Canada after Confederation, that kind of thing."

"Well, well. And you write books in your spare time, like?"

"Mel—" began Eliza.

"That's exactly right, Mel. A definition of academic life. Some of us write books in our spare time, others teach in their spare time. Ah, the dog seems to have adjusted to me. Shall I stand up, see if she responds?" He raised himself to his full height and walked several steps in the direction, but to one side, of Willis. The dog yapped once, then jumped down and trotted over to Eliza, who gestured that it would be all right for Willis to climb up on her lap.

"So that's all right now," Gupta said. "She won't be frightened of wogs from now on."

Charlotte ran out to bring back another pizza. While she was cutting it up, Pickett said, "I'm not sure what I'll do about the cabin. It'll be jinxed for a while as far as the locals are concerned. I'll have to find a summer tenant, someone from the city."

"We could move in ourselves. Rent this place," Charlotte said.

"Then you'd meet *all* my lovers," Eliza said.

It was a complicated signal. Pickett heard a message addressed to him and Charlotte about Eliza's wish for privacy, and guessed a very different one was being sent to Gupta, letting him consider the possibility that he didn't own Eliza. On the other hand, she might just be joking, clearing up the residue from the slight embarrassment at having produced Gupta in the first place.

Pickett said, to change the subject, "Did you ever hear anything or notice anything that would help the OPP?"

"I talked to the sergeant about that. Not very much. Thompson never had any callers, and he didn't own a car, so he used to walk to town and back every day. I did call on him two weekends ago to let him know that I'd pick up anything for him in town, and if he ever needed a cup of sugar, I was there." She looked at Gupta. "That's a traditional gesture in our culture. I was making a sort of joke about days gone by."

"Not a very *good* joke, though, is it?"

Eliza turned back to Pickett. "I remember two or three pickup trucks, the kind half the people in town drive, just on their way somewhere. There was a white one, I remember, came up the road that afternoon, one of those with an engine on the back for welding. And a gray car parked on the shoulder near the highway. I think I'd seen it once before. Actually, it was the usual busy night. People—people in pickup trucks especially—sometimes use your yard to turn around in. And some of them park when no one is home. Someone in the diner once made a joke about Duck Lake Road being the local teenagers' nesting spot. There are also a few quiet lay-bys on the road where they can park for a while; then they turn around and go back to town. You get used to hearing them. And they leave traces of themselves behind.''

"Like what?'' Charlotte asked.

"Like condoms,'' Eliza said. "Safes. It's early in the year and pretty cold, but on Friday, I heard at least three drive in the yard and park for a few minutes. One of them was kids, I would think, by the sound of the broken muffler. You know. *Vroom! Vroom!*''

"You didn't look out and see Thompson at all?'' Pickett asked.

"I looked out once and his light was on, but I never saw any activity. I guess he was already dead by then.''

"Did you get any impression of the guy? Did he seem sad, crazy, manic, drunk? Anything like that?''

"He just seemed like the hired man, answering the door. I couldn't even be sure now what he looked like, he was so ordinary. He did wear suspenders, like a hayseed in an old farm movie, and the top of his forehead was white where his hat came to, but that's all I noticed. Fact is, he looked so much like what you would expect, from pictures and old movies, that he seemed kind of quaint.''

"You said no callers. None?"

"I remember seeing a man standing in the door once, looking as if he was asking for directions. Nobody else.''

"No one ever came at night? He never brought anyone home?"

"No. You know, Mel, I'm the wrong person for this kind of thing. I used to share an apartment in Toronto with a girl who noticed stuff on the street. She could tell you about the life of everyone on the block, just by what she saw from the window. Why? Are you worried about me? Sarwin will protect me, won't you, dear?''

Gupta sipped his beer and leaned back with his legs crossed. ''My ancestors were professional assassins, although we had to give it up when we emigrated to Canada. My family opened a corner store instead. I'm out of practice, but it's still in my genes. The dog can sense it.''

Pickett hung on to the amused tone to judge the seriousness of Gupta's remarks, but withheld judgment on the man generally. He wasn't sure if Gupta was making fun of him or inviting him to share in the fun he was having at someone else's expense, a joke about WASP attitudes toward East Indians.

Eliza said, ''He has a secret wrestling hold known only to people born in the Kashmir.''

"If I can find the right place on his neck, I can subdue a weight lifter with just one thumb and the first two fingers of one hand. Render him unconscious in eleven seconds. Of course he has to lie still while I find the place.''

''That's a Sikh joke,'' Eliza said.

''And that's enough of *that* joke,'' Gupta said.

That was all right, then. It was just love talk, not Gupta getting at him in some way. What Pickett also got from this was that Gupta would be around to look after Eliza when she used the trailer.

Suddenly Charlotte, not quite in the picture, said, ''It's all very well for you to make jokes, but we're not having you in that trailer on your own. If you don't bring someone up with you—'' her eyes swiveled past Gupta and dropped ''—then you have to let us know and we'll move up to the cabin while you're there.''

There was a silence. Charlotte, childless herself, was treating Eliza, a woman almost thirty, as a child, her child. Charlotte realized quickly what she was doing. ''I'm sorry. It's not up to me, is it? You do as you like.'' And then, ''But don't stay up there on your own before they catch this fellow.''

''Or woman,'' Gupta said.

''I don't think so. Norbert Thompson wasn't one for women, as you just said. He never kept company around here. They say his only pleasure was hockey,'' Pickett said.

''Watching it, you mean? On television?'' Gupta asked.

''And listening. On radio.''

''Who are 'they'?''

''They?''

''You said 'they say....' Who are 'they'?''

''The townsfolk,'' Pickett said. ''The customers at

the coffee shop in this case. Charlotte used to work there. She went back this morning for a while."

"The village pump?"

"I suppose so. Though there's the Laundromat, too. But, yeah, you can find out pretty much anything around here if you drink enough coffee. Right, Charlotte?"

"All the gossip," Charlotte agreed. "Shall I make some coffee for us now?"

Gupta said, "They say you make the best coffee in Larch River. That is all I came for."

"Charlotte's the only one around here who doesn't use instant," Pickett said. "Country folk prefer it."

Gupta asked, "Can we hear about the rest of the case? What's happening?"

"They don't know anything yet. I mean Wilkie, the OPP, doesn't."

"Are you involved?"

"I advise them from time to time." He smiled to make sure Gupta realized that he was joking.

"The gray fox," Eliza said.

"Tell us about Norbert Thompson, Charlotte," Gupta said. "Where was he living before?"

"You want all the gossip?"

"Give us about an hour of it now, and the rest by installments."

"Don't be silly."

Pickett watched with amazement as his wife bloomed rosily under the attentions of this handsome dark stranger. She had made no move to make coffee. "Tell Sarwin why Thompson left the chicken farm," he said.

"The story was that she sent him packing."

"Why? Was he a poor worker?"

"Oh, no. He'd run the place by himself for four years, I heard."

"Then did he do something? Did he make unwanted sexual advances to her? Did he neglect to make *wanted* sexual advances? Did he beat her? Did she beat him?"

Eliza said, "When you're from another culture, you can ask questions like that, even if you were born in Edmonton."

Charlotte said, "I don't think he was after her in any of those ways, or her after him. She just didn't need him anymore. It's true, people around here thought that now her husband had passed away, she and Norbert might get together. Some did hint they probably already had, but she put a stop to all that talk by going into Sweetwater and bringing back a husband, a man she'd known for years. Norbert left a week or two later."

"What was the new husband's name? Her name now?"

"Sproat. Aaron Sproat. They met in church. They say now that she'd had an understanding with him for a long time."

"What does 'understanding' mean? Were they lovers?"

Charlotte said, "I never know what that word means anymore. When I was a girl, you used to talk about a pair of young lovers, but it didn't necessarily mean that they were having relations. I think in this case, I would say that yes, they were lovers, but no, they weren't having relations, because it would be against what they believed in. She's very religious. I think they used to have a meal together after church sometimes, waiting for the time they could get together properly. You never really know what goes on between people, though, do you? I don't. The more I think about it, the sorrier I get for her. Not now. Then. She's all right now.''

"Certainly no hanky-panky with Norbert, then?''

"No. No way. Not a chance. At least I don't think so. First, her husband was in the house, and second, they say now that she never showed much liking for Norbert. To a lot of people, he seemed kind of sullen. Some people said he was a bit slow, but Harlan, the man who owns my coffee shop, didn't think so. He says Norbert was underdeveloped—'simple, but not mental' was how he put it. At least no more so than a lot of people Harlan could name. 'Course, everyone around here looks a bit underdeveloped to Harlan; that's why he stays here, to take advantage of them. He's been wheeling and dealing since he was in long pants. He loves a bargain, and he says there's plenty here. He buys up the local rubbish and sells it in Toronto from a stall in the antiques market. You wouldn't believe what people will buy from a stall.''

"Did Thompson save much money? Do they say?'' Gupta asked.

"Harlan got the impression that he had hardly any; that's why he was so pleased to get the cabin. I don't suppose she paid him much. That would be one of the ways he was a bit simple.''

"And while he's been staying in the cabin—what? three, four months?—no one has gotten to know him?''

"Not as far as I know.''

"Still no girlfriend?"

"Not from around here."

"A real bachelor."

"A real hermit, looked like."

There was nothing more to say about Thompson, and in the silence, Eliza offered to help Charlotte with the coffee, which Charlotte seemed to have forgotten. Pickett offered Gupta another drink, but Gupta refused and instead tried to be agreeable to Willis, who sneered at him and dug herself deeper into the couch, making it clear that her tolerance of him was temporary and fragile. Pickett picked the dog up and tried to have a rare anthropomorphic conversation with her, which made Willis so uncomfortable that she jumped out of his arms and followed the women into the kitchen. Soon the women appeared with the coffee, which was quickly finished and applauded, and then the two guests left.

CHARLOTTE, STANDING AT the window, asked, "What do you make of *that*, then?"

"Not much. A few pickup trucks, one with a broken muffler, a welder, a gray car parked on the shoulder. 'Course, she's only been around for a couple of weekends—three?—but you'd think there would be more traffic than that, wouldn't you?"

"I meant *him*. Sarwin."

"Oh, that, yes. Sorry." Pickett had known perfectly well what she meant, but he didn't know yet what he thought, or rather, didn't think anything, so he'd created a diversionary tactic. Charlotte exercised the same prerogative as his first wife, that of asking him immediately what he thought of some new phenomenon—a television play, or as now, a new acquaintance—so that he always had to formulate the first unsophisticated response. The conventional structure of the exchange implied that the superior male wit was being consulted first, but in fact, it was a way of exploiting what looked like the traditional male/female relationship to give her time to think, and something to think against. Pickett had thought this often enough so that he was armed against the question, always saw it coming in time to create a diversion while he tried to discover what he thought he thought.

"Witty fellow, isn't he?" he said.

"You know what I mean."

"Oh, sorry. You mean, what do I think of our Eliza having an Indian boyfriend?"

"You can't call him 'Indian,' can you? Confuses people who grew up near a reservation."

"What'll I call him?"

After some thought, she said, "Nothing."

"You brought it up."

"I know. I'm glad I did, too. Now I know how to deal with the talk in the coffee shop."

"They talking about Eliza and him already?"

"They will be. They'll soon know not to talk in front of me." She looked reflectively out the window. "There's a family in turbans runs a service station about ten miles down the highway, but there aren't any others in Larch River."

"This is a little bit of Old Ontario, Charlotte. No West Indians, no East Indians, no Vietnamese, no blacks; just nice folks like us. No wonder people retire here; they feel like they've come home. It's Ontario fifty years ago. All it needs to be completely authentic is a Chinese restaurant run by the descendants of the coolies who built the railway. But in answer to your first question, I don't think anything, honey. I doubt if they plan to get married yet, but if they do, we've got the name of a counselor, haven't we?"

"What's all this about traffic?" Charlotte asked. "Eliza doesn't seem very safe up there."

"Her thug will look after her."

"Her *what!*" Charlotte glanced at the door in case someone was lurking. "You can't use words like that!"

"Thug? That's what he said he was. An assassin. Thuggee."

"Keep it to yourself, Mel. He was joking, surely. You use that word, everyone in Larch River will know what you think of him."

Pickett sighed theatrically. "I'm too well-read, that's my trouble."

Charlotte said, "Lovely teeth they've got, haven't they?"

"Who?"

"Editors," she said, furious. "Book editors."

EIGHT

In Sweetwater on Monday morning, Sergeant Wilkie said, "Three break-ins, one a week for three weeks, always on Friday night. Why Friday?"

Constable Brendan Copps said, "The TV's bad; there's no hockey. Some people still get paid on Friday. People go shopping in Sweetwater, then stop off for supper. Or they go to the Legion. Friday's a big night at the Legion." He looked at the thing he was eating. "They shouldn't put jam in doughnuts, not first thing in the morning."

"Probably they didn't see a car outside the cabin—Thompson didn't own one—so they went in to help themselves. Then Thompson walked in on them—he had likely been in the village doing his shopping at the IGA—and they panicked. Hit him and killed him, probably by accident."

"Probably. Trouble is, if it was punks, they'll be scared shitless now they've killed someone, so they'll stay home Friday nights for a long time."

"Do you think maybe we're in Newcastle territory? We wondered if they did the Lyles' cabin."

Copps repeated the phrase. "Newcastle territory? What's that? Some 'no-go' area? The body snatchers' domain?"

"It means the area that the Newcastle gang oper-ates in, the break-in boys from Newcastle. You know?''

''Tell me again.''

''There've been a lot of break-ins of summer places in a wide area around Newcastle, but not near New-castle itself, which is why they think the gang oper-ates from Newcastle.''

''Never shit on your own doorstep?''

''No, nothing delicate like that, but a kind of stupid cunning. See, if Newcastle isn't touched, it's because this gang is trying to lay suspicion somewhere else. If they went to only one or two other places, that might work, but now they've been everywhere but Newcastle, so they are doing the opposite of what they wanted. Stupid cunning.''

''Could be cunning cunning. Close to home, some-one might recognize them. But I agree, it's the same, whatever. It puts the finger on Newcastle. So?''

''They started with summer places around Lake Scugog, then began to hit permanent residences. They seemed to have good information about who goes to Florida and when, because all of the owners have been away when they called. They probably scour an area, find a place or two, then come back and hit it. I think they did the Lyles' place.''

''Why?''

''When I reported it to headquarters, they said it fits: nice summer cottage; this time the owner lives in Newcastle, and everybody knows it. They went in, took all his power tools, including his bench saw and generator, all from the tool crib. They didn't touch the cottage proper.''

''Nothing worth taking?''

"Being a summer place, there's no money or jewelry or fur coats. No microwave oven, no TV, no radios, nothing except the furniture, which isn't worth the trouble. And clothes to keep you warm and dry but not worth stealing. The owner spent his money on picture windows and a big stone fireplace, which are hard to steal; he's smart, see, but so are these guys."

"Is this the same guy who supplied us with photographs of everything, showing where it was supposed to be on the walls so he'd know if anything was missing?"

"Serial numbers, the lot. All listed, not that it helped much."

Copps asked, "When was this?"

"A month ago."

"And nothing since?"

"There's been a break-and-enter each Friday since, but they don't look like the work of professionals."

Copps nodded. "It won't be locals at all, unless they're very young kids. The older teenagers will know enough not to operate where they'll be recognized, like the Newcastle gang. Chances are, if they're not total outsiders, they're from Sweetwater." Copps nodded to himself. "Yeah, far enough so they're not known, but they'll know their way around Larch River."

"That the way it goes in the country, Brendan?" Wilkie sat back waiting to get information about small-town ways from his constable, who had grown up, to Wilkie's delight, in a town called South Porcupine. "Tell me about it."

Wilkie was better trained and much more experi-

enced in every area of police work than Copps, but
the constable had the advantage of him in two other
areas: women, and the street smarts he had picked up
in the gutter. Compared to Copps, Wilkie's upbring-
ing had been genteel; he was very much aware that
he lacked the sexual ease Copps had probably acquired in a rural grade school, and he kept the subject
out of their conversation. But he had learned to be
comfortable when Copps talked about petty crime.

Copps said, "You want my life story? Okay. By
the time I was fourteen, I'd lifted every store in Timmins, just down the road from South Porcupine. Two
of us took the bus in every Saturday morning and
loaded up. It was easy."

Wilkie dropped his amused attitude. "You never
got caught?"

"Once, nearly. We were in Bogden's Department
Store and this guy came up behind me close. I was
just going to tell him where to go, and he said, very
quiet, 'They're on to you,' and walked away down
the aisle. When he got to the end, he winked and sort
of wigwagged his head. I said the word to Piggy Pot-
ter—"

"Piggy? Why 'Piggy'?"

Copps grinned. "He looked like a little pig, had a
face like one."

"I thought that maybe in South Porcupine he was
into pigs. A country boy."

"No, no. That was his friend, Hammy. No. Piggy
followed me into the racks of men's raincoats, where
we dumped the stuff we had, except for a couple of
things we'd bought. Piggy didn't want to, but I
pointed out that *someone* had noticed us, the guy who

warned us, so we played it safe. We hung around for a couple of minutes like regular customers, then walked out the door. They picked us up on the sidewalk, but we didn't have a thing on us we didn't have a receipt for. They were very pissed off.''

"Who was the guy who warned you?"

"I think he was trying to pick up boys, but when he saw there were two of us, he didn't bother. Just warned us to show he was on our side. Piggy was kind of ugly, anyway. I was the one who caught the guy's eye."

"So you gave up crime?"

"We had to stop shoplifting Timmins. They knew our faces now. So then four of us took up stealing from cars, from the parking lots. Radios mostly, but anything else we could find. You'd be amazed at how many women leave their purses in their cars. We had a receiver now, a fence, a guy who ran a used-parts shop, mostly secondhand tires, in Iroquois Falls. He gave us a quarter of what the radios were worth."

"And how long did this gang last?"

"A year. Then one night we got chased by a guy who was waiting for us, crouched down in the back seat with a tire iron."

"So *then* you gave up crime."

"Then we started to burgle, back in Timmins."

"You and Piggy?"

"And a couple of others. One of them had a car."

"How long did this go on?"

"Just for the school year. Then, with daylight saving, it was too light to do much."

"Did you do well?"

"It was easy. Yeah."

"So why did you stop?"

"We grew up. Piggy first, I think. He was the most mature. He announced one day that he was quitting. We were just going into grade twelve."

"You never got caught?"

"Like I said, nearly. But not actually, no."

"You'd never be here now if you had."

"That's why we quit. We realized that what they'd been saying all along was true, that we had too much to lose."

"So you all quit?"

"Smokey Stover carried on and got caught six months later."

"What happened to the others?"

"Piggy's a lawyer, works for the provincial government. He'll run in the next election. Herby Benson's a paving contractor—he steals from the government now, building roads."

"And Smokey Stover?"

"On parole, I think. He's habitual. Been in and out ever since."

"Jesus Christ. I had no idea of all the experience we had under our roof."

"Nothing like that ever happened to you? In Toronto, where you grew up?"

"Not that I was involved in. I used to lift apples from the Chinese grocery on my way home from school. Not after ninth grade, though."

"All Boy Scouts, were you?"

"My dad was a policeman. He'd have killed me."

"There it is, then. I didn't have your advantages. I had to find out about right and wrong all by myself. I just made it in time."

"So how about putting your experience to work? How do we find these guys?"

"We'll have to ask around. Leaving out the Newcastle mob, we're probably looking for punks—a couple at least, maybe three or four. We don't know what kind of wheels they have. If it's two of them, it could be anything, but four would be a car. I mean, not a pickup truck. They might have bought gas. One of them might have had a broken muffler. If they borrowed one of their family vehicles, they might've put in gas so that Dad didn't notice how much had been used. They might've stopped to eat something—before, not after. After, they would've wanted to get the hell back to where they came from. Here, probably."

Wilkie thought about what he was hearing, about the crime and about Copps and his Artful Dodger background, and conceded the constable his authority on teenage rural crime. "So you think it's local punks?"

"I didn't say that. I just was telling you how it would be if it *was* punks. That's what you asked. As a matter of fact, if this was a quiz, I would say I don't think so. The kind of punks I ran with wouldn't have hit anybody. We'd've just took off. But who knows? I never got that far. Smokey Stover might've, after a spell in the reformatory. Not when I knew him. But someone hit Thompson from behind, and that says to me that they were not frightened, but maybe real hard cases."

"I think you're right, but they didn't have their own weapon." Wilkie told him about Pickett's discovery of the missing piece of dowel. "I think we'd better cover the local scene, don't you?"

"Oh, sure. Do what they taught us. Try every store that was open then—the coffee shop, the burger shacks, all of them, and the Finger-Lickin' Chicken. We're looking for two or more guys who might have been around for a couple of Fridays. Right?"

"Couldn't be just one guy?"

"Sure. But *we* always went in company when I was a thief, and that's what we're talking about, isn't it? Thieving? One guy on his own means we ought to be looking for some other reason. If you want to include all the possibilities, we're looking for one or more strangers of unknown height, weight, color, and age, seen on this Friday or any other. Not a lot to go on. Any other leads?"

Copps had given Wilkie time to think. "Ask the gas stations for a list of the numbers of cars that bought gas on credit that night. There won't be too many to check."

"Anything else?"

"Find out which of these kids needs a new muffler."

"That it?"

"Find out if there's a welder in town, one with a pickup truck. I guess a welder would *have* to have a pickup truck to carry the generator around, wouldn't he?"

"Sometimes they use a trailer for the generator so they can use the truck for other stuff if they need to. Anything else?"

"Find out more about what Thompson did with his Saturday afternoons."

"He sat in the beer parlor and drank two beers, watching sports on the big screen."

"How do you know?"

"That's what farmers do. They come to town to look at the big screen. What else?"

"I have to talk to Aaron Sproat."

"Who's that?"

"The guy who was courting Mrs. Maguire while her husband was sick."

WHEN WILKIE CALLED him, Sproat asked if they could meet in Sweetwater. "Mrs. Sproat has had enough," he said. He suggested a coffee shop on the main street. "They have those high booths," he said. "It's a little bit private. I could be there in half an hour."

He was a tall, bony man in his early fifties, dressed in clean work clothes. His hair was clipped short well above his ears, and old-fashioned, steel-rimmed glasses completed the look of a farmhand from a previous age, which Wilkie realized he was.

He had been standing by the door of the cafe, waiting for Wilkie—the two men had no difficulty in identifying each other—and when Wilkie walked in, Sproat pointed silently to a booth. Wilkie led the way down the aisle. When they were both seated, Wilkie offered his hand and Sproat looked first at the hand, then at Wilkie's face, then back at the hand before he produced his own to shake. His handshake was literally that, a shaking in which the fingers moved separately from the rest of the hand, as if it was a gesture that Sproat had read about and was now practicing for the first time.

Wilkie ordered coffee for them both, and Sproat raised a finger before the waitress left. "Hold the phone," he said. "I'll have a piece of coconut pie with mine." He added, to Wilkie, "I always eat coconut cream pie when I come here. It's good."

Wilkie nodded, trying to remember the last time he had had a piece of factory pie in a diner like this, waited until the waitress brought the coffee and Sproat's pie, sipped his own coffee and pushed away the cup, pleased to find that it tasted as if it had been stewing since breakfast, if not the day before, as he had anticipated. He waited for Sproat to finish his pie, wondering if the man had the acting skill to conceal any apprehension of the policeman behind the chat about the eating of coconut pie. Probably not, but he might have something to contribute about the victim.

"I'd like to ask you about Norbert Thompson, save bothering your wife too much," he said.

"You already bothered her once. What do you want to know? I know all about him, sure."

"Did you know him long?"

"I didn't know him well personally, except just to speak to. I know all about him from Ruth. My Ruth." He spoke with a declarative belligerence as he looked all around Wilkie, avoiding eye contact.

"How long have you known him to speak to?"

"I met him just after Ruth's first husband died."

"That was the first time? Wasn't he ever around when you called at the farm?"

"I was never a *caller,* mister, until after Mr. Maguire died. Ruth's first husband, that is." Now Sproat looked at him directly to see if Wilkie understood.

"Not once?"

"No, never. Because I had feelings for Ruth, I kept

my distance from her home while her husband was alive."

"But you used to meet her outside the home."

"If you mean somewhere private, the answer to that is no, too."

"But you *did* use to see her."

"I saw her in church, and afterward in here."

To eat the coconut cream pie. "Alone?" he asked. "Just the two of you?"

"Mostly. Anyone was welcome to join us, and sometimes someone did, but most of the time it was just the two of us." The man's voice had a curious mechanically produced quality, as though the words he needed had been separately recorded and were only now being selected and organized into sentences. "I spoke to our minister about my feelings for Ruth to ask him if it was proper we should meet after the service, and he said there was no harm in it as long as I behaved myself. He's a very liberal minister, too much so to my way of thinking."

"How long did you meet after church. Months? Years?"

"About two years."

"You must have got to know each other pretty good."

"Everything that matters. When the time come, we saw no sense in waiting."

"You got married then, and moved up to the farm in...what? Two weeks?"

"Four. The minister said that was enough."

"And Thompson moved out then."

"A couple more weeks. As soon as I had found my way around the farm. It's not complicated, chicken farming, and Ruth knows as much about it as Thompson.''

"Did you get to know him at all in those two weeks?''

"We all et together, but that was all. He wasn't my kind of people, or Ruth's either.''

"What kind was he?''

"To start with, he was a drinker.''

"Heavy?''

"Every Saturday afternoon he'd come back smelling of it.''

"Week after week, eh. Any other bad habits?''

"Like what?''

"Did he play cards, maybe?''

"You trying to make fun of me, mister?''

"No, no. I'm just trying to establish if maybe someone had a grudge. Could be he didn't pay his debts. See what I mean?''

"I see all right.'' Sproat made it clear that he had seen through Wilkie's protest and didn't believe it. Reluctantly, he added, "He only went to town on Saturday afternoons. Nights, he listened to the radio and watched TV. He liked hockey games.''

"Who were his friends?''

"He never brought any back to the farm.''

"Enemies?''

"Never saw any of them, either. He kept out of trouble, kept to himself.''

Wilkie judged that the conversation had recovered from his failure to have a little fun at Sproat's expense, and now he tried to be more man-to-man. "We think he may have interrupted someone trying to rob him, Mr. Sproat. Came home while they were going through his stuff. Did he have anything valuable apart from his TV, do you know?''

''Not that I ever saw. A railway watch was all, but those things aren't valuable, are they?''

''We got that. No. What about money? How did he keep his money, do you know? He left the farm with a few dollars, about six weeks' pay—how much would that have been?''

''You'd have to ask Mrs. Sproat. He got all his meals, and the use of the truck on Saturday afternoons. He didn't need much.''

Wilkie heard a defensive tone in Sproat's reply, and made a note to himself to find out about Thompson's wages. Sproat would know the price of farm labor. So far, it sounded as if Thompson had been a kind of indentured servant.

''One thing, did you ever get the impression that Thompson was a little bit backward? Did Mrs. Sproat ever suggest it?''

''He could read and write, but you didn't catch him doing either very much. No, he was an inward-looking man, but I think he wasn't deficient.''

''It must have been hard on him when you came and he had to go.''

''He didn't have to go. Who said he had to go? He left of his own accord. Just up and left. I suppose I must have had something to do with it, but his going was his own concern. He could have stayed, and I could have carried on delivering feed. I don't really like chickens much. They stink. But I can do it for Mrs. Sproat's sake. No, we didn't send Norbert away. He had a home with us if he wanted. Mrs. Sproat would have seen that as a duty, being nearly kin. She was glad he went, but he could have stayed.''

"Now, something I have to do is find out where everybody was on Friday night. Did you go out?"

Sproat straightened up. "I left Mrs. Sproat to go into Lindsay. I needed to buy some oil for the truck, and it's cheapest at the Canadian Tire store there. I got a receipt, if you want to see it, and I chatted for a couple of minutes with an old customer in the store. If you want, I could get his name."

"That isn't necessary. I'm just filling in the blanks." He nodded and stood up to close the interview. Sproat stayed seated.

As Wilkie moved away, Sproat said, "Catch the waitress, would you? I think I'll have a refill." He held up his cup.

"Another piece of pie?" Wilkie joked.

"I've had my pie," Sproat said. "Just the coffee."

NINE

THE MINISTER LIVED in a small, white-painted house next to the church. A sign—no more than a label—over the door of the church said it was the First Gospel Church. There was no notice board indicating the time of services or the minister's name.

"We call ourselves the First Gospel Church of Sweetwater, though there isn't any Second. We are the only congregation in the county, and we aren't affiliated with any others outside."

"Mrs. Sproat said you had split off from the other…congregations? Why was that? Was there a quarrel?"

"They wanted more ritual. We wanted none of it. Now they're talking about joining up with the United people. Next will be the Anglicans, then Rome. But our faith is based on the Bible, not on a lot of edicts from a pope. The word of God unadorned. We don't hold with organs, either. There aren't any organs in the Bible. Or guitars, for that matter."

"When do you hold your services?"

"We meet Sunday mornings and evenings. Why?"

"I thought I might drop by."

"Why?"

Wilkie had not anticipated this. "I was just interested."

"What in?"

"What you had to offer."

"Don't you subscribe to any faith?"

"I think my wife is Anglican."

"Then ask your wife to take you to church. Don't bother to come to ours. We don't like tourists."

"We live here."

"There are different kinds of tourists. What I mean is that we aren't on show. We get together to worship God. Try the Anglicans, they put on a good show. I hear they're using incense now."

"So you are on your own. I suppose the other churches would call you strict?"

"We practice the faith that they preach."

"Did Norbert Thompson ever attend your church?"

"Never. I remember asking Mrs. Maguire, as she was called then, to encourage him to come along, but she said he wasn't interested. To tell you honestly, Inspector..." The minister looked unsure of himself for a moment.

"Sergeant."

"Sergeant. I don't think she tried very hard. I think he must have been quite a good man—hard worker and all that—but Mrs. Maguire was more strict than the rest of us. You see, she used to be Cotterite, and when that sect died out, she came over to us. But on her own, in her house, she kept up the Cotterite faith."

"What would that involve? This is all new to me."

"I can tell that. You have to have grown up here. Hubert Cotter broke away from the Baptists when some of them joined up with the United Church...

what? Seventy years ago? But he was more…er, what?—purist?—than the *other* Baptists who broke off, and he started his own congregation. Time took care of it, though; it's gone now. But Mrs. Maguire kept the faith. No cooking on Sundays, that sort of thing. I found out just how literalist she was when she came to me to see if it was all right for her to have a cup of coffee once a week with Aaron Sproat.'' For a few words, the minister sounded slightly incredulous about what he was saying, but his orthodoxy prevailed and he brushed aside the apparent temporary apostasy. ''I gave them my blessing, as long as they met in public.'' Suddenly, urgently, he burst out, ''It was the only relief the poor woman got. Coffee once a week with Sproat. She was doing nothing wrong in her heart. The rest of the time, she lived with a sick husband and a man she detested.''

''Detested?''

Now the minister looked confused. He bowed his head. ''I'm sorry. You're right. That was too strong. But when you asked me if Thompson had ever come to church, I wasn't quite straight with you. Thompson came to see me once, to find out if it would be all right if he attended services. I discouraged him, even though he was family-connected. Mrs. Maguire had already mentioned that he wanted to join us—that he had asked her. I don't think he realized that she didn't like him. Of course, a more likely reason is that he would have had to ride back and forth with her in the truck every Sunday morning, and then her little coffee get-together with Aaron Sproat would have been affected. So I discouraged him. Mrs. Sproat is one of our…I couldn't afford to lose her. Taking one thing

with another, I think I did right. He just needed somewhere to worship, and it would have been divisive to
have him with us. Anyway, he was doing his Christian duty by sitting with his brother while she came
to church. Otherwise, she would have had to stay
home herself. She's a very good woman, but..."

"But what?"

"Sir, a man like you doesn't have the right to know
the problems of keeping to the true faith, what it's
like for a real Christian."

"So tell me."

The minister looked at Wilkie with contempt.
"You haven't the slightest idea of what I'm talking
about, have you?"

"That sounds kind of arrogant. For a Christian."

The minister flushed. "All right, I'll try you. Ob-
serving our congregation, I have come to the conclu-
sion that there is a process always at work turning
faith into dogma. A church like ours—all churches in
the beginning—starts with revelation, but then it lays
down an order of service so that the congregation
doesn't have to create it every week. The form of the
service is the letter, not the spirit, but inevitably in
time the letter becomes more important than the spirit,
and then it becomes necessary for some to regain the
spirit—I'm trying to talk in a language you would
understand. Do you?"

"I think so. You're finding your own congregation
a bit rigid. Right?"

The minister shrugged and said nothing. Then,
"Anything else?"

"Just...good luck."

BEFORE HE CHECKED the Sweetwater beer parlors that Thompson might have patronized on his Saturday afternoons off the farm, Constable Copps did the rounds of the few stores in Larch River.

Along the highway, many of the small businesses that existed to serve the summer trade—the soft-ice-cream bars, the live-bait shops, the doughnut counters, and the chip wagons—had not yet opened for the season. Of those that were open, none could report any significant sightings of strangers on Friday afternoon or evening. He had more luck in town; the assistant in the hardware store offered a list of possibilities, including ''a guy who was around on the Friday a week before, inquiring after whoever built the cabin—Mr. Pickett. This guy was wanting to build one of his own, and he wanted to talk to Mr. Pickett because he'd heard about the one he'd put up. I told him where to find the cabin, and that if no one was there, then Mr. Pickett's granddaughter would probably let him have a look at the cabin.''

''Who?''

''Mel Pickett's granddaughter. She came out from England and he lets her use the trailer.''

''That's not his granddaughter. She's somebody else. I know her. She lived here last summer while they put on that play.''

''I wasn't here then. Somebody told me she was his granddaughter.''

''Somebody's mixing them up. You're mixing them up.''

''Well, who's with the Pakki, then? The granddaughter or the other one?'' The assistant grinned. ''Or both?''

"Who's this Pakki?"

"An Indian guy who spends time in the trailer. They were talking in the beer parlor about him the other day."

"What were they saying?"

"Siggy Siggurdson said he could stay in Larch River as long as he behaves himself."

"Who would he use as a model? Siggy?"

"What?"

"Never mind. You remember anyone else hanging around? You've got a good view from this window. You ought to rent chairs."

"We're starting to see some tourists, people driving around looking for a restaurant. And people looking for a summer cabin come in here a lot. But I don't remember anyone special, and the guy wanting to see the cabin never came back."

"Do you remember anything about him?"

"He was a young guy, about thirty, but he'd been in the wars, so his age was hard to tell."

"You mean been in a lot of fights?"

"Something like that. He had six or seven scars on his face, and no teeth up top. I think he was probably a hockey player. You know, like one of those guys in the Paul Newman movie, playing in the American League, old guys, over thirty, stretching out their last few years."

"Did you see what he was driving?"

"An old pickup. A white one. There was someone else with him. I never saw him, but I remember the hockey player waving through the window at someone sitting outside, as if whoever he was with might be getting impatient. But the first guy was the driver.

Yeah, when he went out to the truck, he got in on the driver's side and whoever it was moved over.''

From the hardware store, Copps moved on to Harlan's motel and beer parlor, where the waiter assured him that Thompson never patronized the place. Before he left Larch River, Copps remembered to ask Harlan, as the owner of the gas pump outside the diner and of the gas station on the highway, to provide the police with a list of all the license numbers on the credit cards that had been used on Friday. Copps didn't expect much from this; punks, in his experience, used cash when they were on a job.

From Larch River, he drove back to Sweetwater to check the three beer parlors that Thompson might have used. Thompson's death was now an item in Sweetwater gossip, and in the first beer parlor he called on, the waiter knew all about the dead man.

"He used to come in here every Saturday afternoon—I mean right up to last week. He sat at the same table every week and drank two beers, no more, no less, every week. Then he'd have his supper over at the Chew'n'Chat, and pick up his laundry, and that was it. The big afternoon out.''

"Did he have any buddies here?''

"Once in a while you'd see him shooting the shit with a couple of senior citizens, two-beer types themselves, but they just talked about what was playing up there.'' He pointed to the TV screen. "He didn't come here to meet them, no.''

They remembered Thompson in the Chew'n'Chat, a sandwich-and-fries restaurant that also offered steaks, chops, and liver and onions. The meals came with potatoes, green beans, and gravy. "He always had a steak," the owner/waitress said. "And a piece of pie à la mode."

"Was he always by himself?"

"Always."

THE WOMAN WHO RAN the Laundromat wrung her hands and smiled too much for someone with all her wits about her. She dressed like an old woman, but Copps thought she was no more than forty. She had a pleasant face in spite of her smile, and a smallish frame, but a bosom of a size Copps associated with sopranos; it was a feature she seemed to want to conceal with her wringing hands.

She, too, knew that Thompson was dead. When Copps introduced himself, she shook her head and locked onto Copps' eyes, bonding in sympathy.

"He did his laundry here?" Copps asked, pointing at the row of machines.

"I did it," she said. "See, he used to take his shirts to the Sentinel Cleaners and they charged him a dollar fifty a shirt, and when he told me that, I offered to iron them for him. So it became a regular thing. He'd bring in his dirty laundry and give me enough change for the machine, and I'd give him back the clean things from the week before." She smiled and smiled, and dropped her hands slightly, relaxing as she talked. "It wasn't much of a job. He was such a clean man. *So* clean."

Copps smiled at her. "I need some shirts ironed."

She ducked her head, avoiding his smile. "I just did them as a favor for him. He didn't have anyone else. I'll bet *you* do."

"Special, was he?"

"He was a nice man."

"So you said. Did you ever see him with anybody? Any friends?"

She shook her head.

"He ever talk to you about himself?"

"Only about how many chickens they had killed that week, and the eggs they sold."

"Not too lively."

"Nothing wrong with that." Her face closed down.

It was an odd response, requiring an effort to connect it with what they had been saying. Was she defending Thompson's dullness, or talking about her own preference for a quiet life? Whatever it was, he had put her off for the moment, so he thanked her for her time, and left.

Finally he called in at Sweetwater's muffler shop, The Quiet Man, to find out who had had his truck repaired since Friday. He got three names, and left behind instructions that he wanted to know if any more turned up needing mufflers. On his way out, he remembered the welding truck.

"There's none in Larch River," the owner of the muffler shop assured him. "They get any welding they want done here in Sweetwater, either by McCormack or Fred Grange."

"Which one drives a white pickup?"

"Neither. One's blue, dark blue, and the other's black."

TEN

THAT MORNING, Pickett told Charlotte he wanted to do something about Eliza's safety, explaining that he planned to fix floodlights by the cabin that would be triggered by anyone coming through the property. It had been on his list for some time, but now he used Thompson's death to push it to the top.

Charlotte said, "Can you get them in Sweetwater?"

"I think I have to go in to Toronto. There's a specialty place on St. Clair where I can take my pick. I could waste an hour in Sweetwater and two in Lindsay and still not get what I need. This place has it for sure."

"You'll be gone all day then?"

"You nervous about being on your own?"

"I've lived in this house for twenty-five years, ten of them on my own. But you be back by dusk, so I'll know how to time dinner. Call me if you're going to be done earlier."

"If I *am* finished early, I'll stop in on Wilkie in Sweetwater. See if there's any news."

"I thought you might."

He could see she thought that was the real reason for him driving to town—so he could pass through Sweetwater and talk to Wilkie. His story was thin; the fact was that he could have bought everything he needed two hundred yards away from the house, in the hardware store in Larch River, which did a good business selling alarm systems to summer cottagers, and he prepared a refined version of his story just in case Charlotte told someone in the coffee shop about his errand and they put her straight. But he was glad she didn't believe him anyway; it was as if he wasn't lying after all.

He did call on Wilkie in Sweetwater first, hoping that the sergeant might already have arrested a local man, but there was no news. His instinct was not to tell Wilkie what errand he was on, without giving that instinct much thought; thus when Wilkie inquired, he told him the same story about buying floodlights as he had told Charlotte.

IN TORONTO, none of his old colleagues was working the day shift in the Bail-and-Parole Unit except for Sergeant Marinelli, but Pickett found that he was known to everyone, having become a legend: "Pickett the Pioneer." His log cabin intrigued them and had come to form an important part of his image for them. The pattern was familiar: first the jokes, then the questions about did he *really* build it himself. When they were all satisfied, he got to cross the street for a quiet cup of coffee with his old crony, Marinelli, to whom he explained the problem.

Ever since he had seen the picture of the body on the floor of the cabin, he had been troubled by the notion that at first glance, it looked like himself on the floor, simply because that was who you expected to find on the floor of his cabin. And that had got him wondering if the killer had not simply expected to find him at home, and from that, Pickett had gone on to the possibility that he was the intended victim. He kept in front of his mind the near certainty that Thompson had been killed by an intruder who had been disturbed in the act of burgling the cabin, but he nevertheless could not blot out the recurring image, like a still photograph flashing in his head, of himself dead on the floor of the cabin; it was an image that seemed to be warning him, because if by the remotest chance, it *was* him who was supposed to have been killed, then perhaps the killer would return as soon as the news of Thompson's death was published, or at some time thereafter come again to look for Pickett.

The possibility was slight, but he did not think that considering it indicated paranoia. He might have shrugged off the risk to himself, but he felt that the safety of Charlotte, and even of Eliza, was at risk, so he had driven in to Toronto. He'd bought the flood-lights and some alarm equipment and then driven over to the Bail-and-Parole Unit, for it was his idea that if he *was* the intended victim, then the largest pool of possible assailants was made up of all the criminals he had helped put away over the years he had been in Homicide, all of whom would have to report to the Bail-and-Parole Unit when they got out. He could think of half a dozen who had cursed him at some point, usually right after sentencing, and promised revenge. His reaction, the reaction of all policemen, was to tell them to join the queue. Their desire for revenge never survived the jail term. But this might be the exception.

Marinelli asked, ''You have any ideas?''

''Not yet. I helped put away my share of them

when I was in Homicide, and before that, there were a few assault cases, drug dealers—you know. Any one of them could be bearing a grudge.''

"You feeling spooked?''

"A little bit. It's a possibility is all, and it always is. But this is not just for me. I've got a house trailer up there I used when I was building the cabin. There's a girl, a woman, uses it weekends. And I got married again, did you know?''

Marinelli grinned. "We heard.''

Pickett could guess at the jokes that had been trotted out at his expense. He waited for Marinelli to decide not to try one now. Then he said, "So I want to know if anyone is still looking for me.''

"We can check the circulars in the office.''

Pickett nodded. A circular was distributed whenever the system released a criminal with a history of violence, especially if he had been heard swearing revenge while in prison. "That would be a start,'' he agreed.

"Apart from that, if there *is* someone, we wouldn't necessarily know, would we? We handle the records for most of them, but if the parole officer is federal, they wouldn't come into us.''

"Let me see what you've got.''

They went back to the unit, passing the lineup of people on bail or parole who were required to report once a week. As many as six hundred a day went through the office.

Pickett thumbed through the circulars first, but he remembered none of the names. Then he glanced at the records that Marinelli produced, but once more there were no familiar names.

"Sorry, Mel, or, I guess, no, that's good, isn't it?"

"I guess so." Pickett stood up. "It's a start. Thanks."

They shook hands and Pickett left, watched on his way out by the lineup of criminals.

The expedition was completed well before noon, and Pickett had the time he wanted to drive across town to his house on Alcorn Avenue. He'd planned to drive down about once a week while it was empty during the summer, to cut the grass and generally make sure the place was intact. His neighbor, a librarian, would keep his porch free of flyers, and she had Charlotte's phone number in Larch River if the place caught fire, but she would not know if the plumbing had sprung a leak, or if someone had quietly broken in through the back door. And he had had no tenant on the second floor since his granddaughter Imogen had gone home to England.

Before he had conceived the plan to build a cabin, before he had met Charlotte, he had satisfied his need to make and build things by remodeling the house, duplexing it into upper and lower units. Downstairs, he turned the former dining room into a shower and a den; he kept a couch in the den for overnight visitors, and a television set because he was old-fashioned enough not to want a blank eye staring at him in the living room when he was trying to read. He had moved his own bed into the basement.

On the second floor, he had carved a self-contained, one-bedroom apartment out of the former three bedrooms and bathroom, completing the conversion by boxing in the stairs and putting a door at the foot of the stairs. At first he had rented the second floor to married students, keeping the rent low in exchange for mild dog-sitting duties—his librarian neighbor did the serious dog-sitting when he went to England—and some caretaking when Pickett was away, chiefly in the long, bleak period from Christmas to Easter.

Then, when his long-forgotten "granddaughter" appeared on his doorstep, he had made it easy for her to stay by offering her the second-floor flat, and so, finally, he had had all the pleasures of having a granddaughter to love without any of the anxieties of raising children along the way. The fact that she was not his granddaughter, not related to him in any way, and the further fact that she looked like her grandmother at her age—the girl Pickett had fallen in love with in 1944—made the nature of his fondness for the girl complicated, even suspect, as he knew perfectly well without letting it worry him. Most people see likenesses to the family in their grandchildren; Pickett saw the likeness to his first love, and enjoyed it.

But Imogen had returned to England, and now Pickett found a letter from his "son," Imogen's father, in the mailbox, an answer to his query about how he felt about Pickett's desire to adopt him legally so that Pickett's estate would go to him, to be held in trust for Imogen and her sister. For nothing was simple: If the world was to believe that Pickett was Imogen's natural grandfather, then the same would have to be true of her sister. Slowly, Pickett read the letter.

Dear Mr. Pickett,

Already I am having trouble writing this. I realize I ought to call you "Father," but I can't do that, not at the moment, so "Mr. Pickett" it will have to be.

Your letter astonished me, although Imogen talks about you continually. You seem to have looked after her well while she was in Canada, and I thank you for that. But I must tell you my own feelings about you have not changed, so I think it fair to warn you of that before I come, which is what I have decided to do, to meet you face-to-face and have it out with you.

You can hardly expect me to welcome the idea of being adopted by a stranger, a foreigner, and at my age, can you? I grew up believing you seduced my mother, abandoned her to have me in secret, and although I know you saw her once or twice more, and I admit she always spoke well of you, nevertheless you washed your hands of her and of me. Of course, after I was old enough to realize what you had done, I was happy never to see you or to hear of you again.

However, Imogen's initiative has complicated matters, and now this proposal of yours looks to benefit her and her sister substantially, and I don't have the right to dismiss it out of hand. But I'm not jumping with joy over it. Everyone knows the facts of my bastardy, and these days it is no great thing. I have lived perfectly comfortably with the known situation; I don't share Imogen's romantic obsession with discovering our origins. I am a happy bastard, and I don't know that I want to change. But let me come to my real objection.

What I have written so far omits one thing,

something that changes everything. I have lately learned something about you that Imogen does not know, and I am not sure I should tell her, but it bears on our relationship so directly as to render nugatory everything I have said so far. So I am coming over, and so is Imogen. We shall arrive separately—I have business in New York with our head office, and I will be staying at the Plaza Hotel, in case you want to get in touch before I come. But I plan to arrive in Toronto early in the week of the 18th of April. Imogen will fly from here and we will meet in Toronto. I will be in touch later.

Pompous bastard, Pickett thought. He looked up "nugatory" and felt a chill of apprehension, then confirmed from the calendar that his "son" would be arriving next week. Christ! And Imogen. He would have to bring Charlotte down to Toronto to meet her bastard of a stepson. He dialed the number of the Plaza Hotel in New York and learned there was no one staying there called Colwood. The letter had been written on the English company's letterhead, and after a bit of calling around, Pickett got the number of the New York head office and found the man his son had come to New York to see. Apparently they had concluded their business very quickly, and as far as the New York executive could remember, the son was now touring New England before going up to Canada to join some distant relative.

There was nothing for Pickett to do, therefore, except to leave a message with his neighbor that if she saw someone standing on his doorstep with a suitcase, she should direct him to Larch River. At least give him Charlotte's number. He would know about the cabin; Imogen had visited the site in earlier days.

ELEVEN

AFTER PICKETT LEFT, Wilkie gave him a few minutes to get clear of the town and then drove into Larch River. He had no secrets from Pickett as far as the Norbert Thompson case was concerned, but he was glad to know Pickett was out of the way, because he wanted to chat to the bank manager about Thompson without anyone else listening; most of all, he wanted to give the bank manager the sense that their chat was completely off the record. He didn't want the manager looking up and seeing Pickett waving outside the window.

Ernie Villiers, the manager of the only branch of a bank in Larch River, regarded the confidentiality of his customers' financial affairs as sacred, at a certain level. That is, he would not have dreamed of being indiscreet about one of the townspeople's banking interests to another. But Wilkie knew he had been a very useful source of information in the last case, when he had allowed Pickett to know about what seemed like the odd banking behavior of one of his customers who was connected to the case. By tracing a sum of money that ought to have been deposited in the customer's account, Pickett had helped Wilkie unravel a thread that started off the solution to the crime. It now occurred to Wilkie that Villiers might know something interesting about Norbert Thompson, but first Wilkie had to show himself a man to be trusted.

He introduced himself and made his first mistake. "You were very helpful to us in nailing Timmy Cullen," he said.

Villiers looked blank. "I don't remember speaking to you at all, Sergeant. And I don't remember this bank being asked to testify at the trial. You caught the man with a gun hiding in Betty Cullen's basement, I heard. And then Mel Pickett figured it all out, I understand, though maybe Lyman Caxton, our own cop, got there at the same time. *You* guys thought it was Siggy Siggurdson, I heard."

"That the way the story goes? We *all* knew it was Timmy Cullen. But Mel knew where to find him."

"And Lyman."

"Lyman Caxton knew he was in the basement, too, yes."

"The newspaper report didn't read that way."

"We simplified it so the lawyers wouldn't screw it up in the courtroom. And so we wouldn't have to charge Lyman with failure to cooperate."

"Made you look good, though, simplifying it. I'm surprised you haven't made inspector out of it."

The malice behind Villiers' comments nearly made Wilkie give up. But before he could speak, Villiers continued. "Personally, I'm glad you simplified it, even though Mel didn't get the credit he was due."

"He's retired, he doesn't need it."

"I don't either, and I'm not retired. I was happy to hear there was no mention of how you caught up with Siggy."

"We wouldn't have brought that in anyway. All

we would have had to say was how we were suspicious of Siggy's spending spree. It's normal police procedure after a robbery in a small community to wonder why someone has suddenly got rich.''

"Timmy didn't appeal, did he? I mean, he won't now, will he?''

"He'd be too late.''

Villiers nodded. "Sleeping dogs, then. So what are we talking about now? Norbert Thompson? Yes, he banked here. You might have found that out from anyone. The account is frozen now, of course, until someone tells me what to do.''

"I understand.''

Villiers said nothing for a while, then, "Did Mel tell you what I told him about that bakery account?''

"I don't remember. If he did, it's gone now. It never became material after we found Timmy.''

"Ah.'' He nodded. "Water under the bridge then, is it? So. What do you want to know?'' Villiers eased himself in his chair and leaned back.

"Nothing about Thompson's account. More about your impression of his situation on that chicken farm, and after he left it.''

Villiers took a few moments to think about the question. "I wondered about that myself. As I understood it, he couldn't collect unemployment insurance because he'd never paid in, nor did his brother for him. Apparently he worked on some kind of contract. Day laboring, only by the month.''

"How much does a hired man make around here?''

Villiers grinned. "Hired *what?*'' He spluttered and giggled and hissed with glee in anticipation of what he was going to say. "About as much as a swineherd, I would think. Bit less than a dairymaid."

"What are you talking about?"

"What are *you* talking about? I'll ask around for you, but I've not heard the term 'hired man' in years. As I say, like 'dairymaid,' and 'swineherd' and 'plowboy.' I'll see if anyone else has. Hold on."

Villiers looked up a number in his book and called it; then, obviously speaking to a friend, he went into a conversation to establish the going rates for a hired man. He put the phone down. "That was a pal of mine who runs a hobby farm near Peterborough. He says there aren't any hired men these days. They call them 'farm managers,' pay them a thousand a month and give them a house rent-free."

Wilkie saw a way to dismantle the last of Villiers' caution and unleash the banker's natural desire to share his understanding of the natives with another administrator. "Are we talking confidentially, Mr. Villiers?"

"Of course." Villiers glowed. He got up and made sure the door was shut. "Mel will vouch for me on that score," he said.

"He did already. You don't know what they paid Thompson?"

Villiers, slightly irritated at being asked something when he had thought he would be hearing a bit of gossip, said, "No, I don't. Probably ten dollars a week and all the bullcock sandwiches he could eat."

"All the what?"

"Bullcock. What they make baloney sausage out of. Bulls' cocks. And they got rid of him as soon as he wasn't wanted. Fucking Bible-thumpers. You religious, Sergeant?''

"I don't go to church."

"Nor do I. Nor do I. I was a Catholic once, but I couldn't keep up with all the sins I was committing. After my wife left me, I let them get on with it, and I've enjoyed whatever's come my way since. Enjoyed it all,'' he repeated, making sure Wilkie understood. "I'll pay for it one day, but all the same, better a lapsed Catholic than one of these teetotalitarian sourbellies."

"You know about them, Mr. Villiers?"

"Ernie. Don't we all? Isn't this a case? I often wondered about Norbert Thompson, how much they paid him, because he didn't deposit much with us. Most weeks, all he had was dribs and drabs; some weeks, nothing at all. Jesus Christ. He probably didn't earn enough to change his oil."

"He didn't have a car or truck of his own."

"*His* oil, Sergeant, not the truck's." Villiers winked to drive the point home.

"Yeah, right," Wilkie said eventually, wondering if Copps had heard that one. "Help me do the sums, Ernie. He drank two beers every Saturday afternoon, ate a steak dinner for about fifteen dollars, got his hair cut, bought the odd bit of clothing. He didn't own a car, and he had no hobbies that we can find evidence of in the cabin. Now, you know what he deposited here—no, no—don't tell me, just figure it in. Would you say there's a sum of money unaccounted for?"

Villiers inserted a corner of a match folder between two of his lower side teeth while he considered the implications of answering the question. "If they paid him more than fifty a week, you mean? You mean there could be a considerable sum lying about somewhere?''

"Could *have* been, either in some other account, or in his safe-deposit box here or...I don't know.''

"Hidden in the woodpile where Siggy hid his?''

"We found Siggy's under the mattress.''

"That's right. It was Mel Pickett's chain saw you found in the woodpile. Right?''

Wilkie nodded, waiting for Villiers to feel his way back to the real question.

Villiers said, "What happened to the rest of the money that Siggy found on the body?''

"We confiscated it.''

"I know that. What happened to it?''

"You'd have to ask the Provincial Attorney-General's Office. They handle things like that.''

"You didn't leave it with Siggy?''

"Just the bit he'd spent. We didn't ask for it back. Siggy's chief reward was that he knew he had been a good citizen.''

Villiers laughed. "That's how Siggy tells it, too, in Harlan's beer parlor. So. No, I don't believe that Norbert Thompson was the kind of man who would even rent a safe-deposit box. He was a very simple fella.''

Willie nodded. "You think I might be right then, about some money going begging somewhere?''

"I see what you're getting at. Yes, he could have been robbed. Put it like that, if they paid him a living wage, he could have accumulated a tidy little nest egg over the years. But if he did, why didn't he deposit it here?''

"He was a strange man. Maybe he didn't want your tellers to know about his affairs."

"Me, you mean. Well, it's a small town. The only other thing I can think of is that he spent it all on lawyers." Villiers leaned away from the desk, no longer having to be careful of what he said. "He and I talked about it one day, when he first came here to live, and I started to notice him occasionally at the wicket. I asked him in to the office—I do that just in case one of these farmers strikes oil on his corn patch; then it's my job to get to him before the other sharks move in and advise him. Anyway, the first and only time we talked, he asked me to recommend a lawyer to him. I asked him how big his problem was—you know, being nosy. I said there were different kinds of lawyers for different classes of work. Was it a will he needed? He said it was his rights he was concerned with. Wanted to sue someone. So I gave him the name of a couple of lawyers in Sweetwater who like being in court, and that was that. But you know, I think he was brooding. It seemed to me he was just sort of waking up to how he'd been screwed."

"So why did he do it for four years?"

"As I say, I think he had been asleep. When they let him go, he woke up. Now, I've got work to do. So have you. You find out that they were paying Thompson a real wage and you've got a puzzle to unpick. But I'll tell you, it makes just as much sense—no, more sense—to figure they probably only paid him fifty a week."

TWELVE

"WHAT'S ON YOUR MIND, Mel?"

They were in Wilkie's office. It had seemed to Pickett like a good idea to see if the sergeant had found out anything he could report to Charlotte, to divert her from asking him what he had been doing in the city. But somehow his apparently casual inquiry had sounded loaded. Wilkie had made a solemn business of taking Pickett into an inner office, closing the door and pouring coffee before asking the question, so that Pickett would know this was important.

Pickett rubbed his nose with a thumb and a finger, quieting an itch, and told him.

Wilkie said, "That's what I figured. The idea occurred to me, too. I mean, the idea that you looked a bit like the guy in the picture, or rather, that someone who didn't know you, seeing a guy lying on the floor of your cabin, might think it was you. I didn't make the second jump, though, that someone else had actually come looking for you, and seeing the other guy alive, made the same mistake. I think it's a little farfetched, but then, I don't look like the guy in the picture." Wilkie sipped his coffee. "So, you feeling nervous?"

"I figure it wouldn't hurt to fix up a couple of good trip lights." This was the point at which Pickett might have mentioned his visit to the Bail-and-Parole Unit, but he stayed silent.

"We did turn up someone who was looking for the cabin that afternoon." And he told Pickett the story of the over-the-hill hockey player who had wanted to find out how to build a cabin. "You know anyone like that?"

Pickett shook his head, troubled by his lie of omission, but only to the extent of not wanting to be caught out. "Trouble is, that cabin has made me famous in these parts." And then, as if the idea had just occurred to him, "Suppose they were after me? What happens when the news about Thompson gets out? Will they come back looking for me?"

"Take it easy. To start with, this is just you thinking the picture in the cabin looks like you."

"Eliza's on her own up in the trailer sometimes."

Wilkie frowned. "Eliza? Yeah, right. I thought she was shacked up with some Indian guy. That's what the whole town thinks. East Indian, not an Ojibwa."

"Sometimes she's shacked up with some Indian guy and sometimes she isn't. And that's another possibility. I don't like the idea of punks in pickup trucks looking for some excitement. What are the statistics on racism around here? I know your general crime rate is pretty high, but how are you fixed for the Klan, or the Hitler Youth, or whatever they call themselves? Any assholes like that around?"

"Okay, okay. We *have* sighted two pickup trucks driving around."

"One of them driven by an old hockey player? Or do you mean two *other* pickup trucks?"

"Just two, probably including the hockey player.

But we've got one other license number. Seems someone paid for some gas in brand-new twenties, so the girl wrote the license number on the back just in case they made them themselves. And there's a gray Chevrolet acting strange.''

"Eliza noticed him. Probably a bird-watcher. You found anyone local who might have had it in for Thompson?''

"People around Larch River hardly knew him. He did odd jobs that he got through Harlan.''

"Didn't he socialize?''

"Only on Saturday afternoons in Sweetwater. The same as when he lived on the farm. Two beers a week and a steak dinner at the Chew'n'Chat.''

"What about the farm? Was there any bad blood between Thompson and his sister-in-law, or her new husband?''

Wilkie told Pickett of what he had learned from Sproat about the lack of any relationship between Thompson and Mrs. Sproat.

Pickett said, ''You think she and this guy Sproat were lovers all the time her husband was sick? And Thompson didn't know?''

"They were a pair, all right, but not like the two up in your trailer. They had a cup of coffee and a piece of coconut pie together once a week after church for about two years. That's it. These are very, very religious people. They even got the minister's okay to have their coffee together.''

"So what made them a pair?''

"They themselves probably didn't think they were a pair, until her husband died. They would be operating under a big taboo, I would think. After her husband finally was gone, they realized they had been courting for two years and they got married in four weeks. With the minister's blessing. You belong to a church?''

''No.''

Wilkie nodded, released from having to be careful. ''I kind of liked the minister.''

''All this sounds like Norbert Thompson having a good reason to kill Sproat, or even Mrs. Sproat, not the other way around.''

''That's what I said. But Norbert Thompson lived a pretty simple life, and I don't have many places to look. We've found where he used to drink his two beers on Saturday afternoons, sometimes with a couple of other guys. They talked about hockey or baseball, but he never seemed interested in a game of hearts up at the Legion, anything like that. He sounds a little bit retarded to me. Not mentally, emotionally.''

''You've been talking to that psychiatrist again. And that's it? That all the gossip?''

''Except for the guy in the gray Chevy, and a welder.''

Pickett stood up. ''This hockey player, how did you run across him?''

''The guy in the hardware store mentioned him.''

''Did he know me? The hockey player?''

''No. No, the hardware guy mentioned you to him. Apparently he had heard about your cabin, but he didn't know you.''

''See? I'm a tourist attraction.''

FIFTEEN MINUTES LATER, Wilkie followed Pickett to Larch River, but drove on through the town until he came again to the Sproats' place.

The chicken farm still looked like a prisoner-of-war camp during a rest period. Only the dogs testified to the presence of life inside, but when they came forward, barking, the door opened and Aaron Sproat stood there. Something about him suggested that he saw himself as the guardian of the keep. He called the dogs to him, and Wilkie climbed out of the car and approached.

"I need a word with Mrs. Sproat," he said.

"What for?"

"*Mrs.* Sproat," Wilkie repeated, letting Sproat know that he didn't plan to explain himself.

Sproat stepped back and let him by.

"I won't need you," Wilkie said.

"I'm staying anyways. Mrs. Sproat might want me."

"You'll stay out of our talk, though, won't you?"

The level of hostility was escalating as Wilkie tried to irritate Sproat, to find out if there was more behind his attitude than ordinary protectiveness.

"Mrs. Sproat's my wife."

"I know that, sir. I'm not here to arrest anyone, just to ask a couple of questions. So stay if you like, but don't speak until I ask you to, okay?"

They moved into the living room, where Mrs. Sproat was already seated at the table on one of the straight-backed chairs. Wilkie took a chair opposite and Sproat sat between them, on one side, with his arms crossed.

"We've been trying to establish why anyone would want to kill someone as harmless as Norbert Thompson," Wilkie began. "Find a motive." He addressed himself directly to Mrs. Sproat.

"We heard it could've been an accident," Sproat said. "He could've fell against the stove."

Wilkie turned sharply and cut in on the last word. "That's the free one, sir," he said. "You don't get any more of those. Speak up once more and we'll go into Sweetwater, where your wife and I can talk in private. Suit yourself."

Sproat laced his hands over his crotch and leaned back, silent.

"How much did you pay Thompson, Mrs. Sproat?"

Without actually speaking, Sproat, by stiffening his back, turning his head, snorting softly, then shifting his chair, made it clear that Mrs. Sproat was dealing with a loaded question. Wilkie ignored him, keeping his eyes on Mrs. Sproat.

"Who needs to know?" she asked.

"Huh?"

"Who needs to know? Why?"

"How much did you pay him, ma'am?"

"A hundred a week."

Sproat let out a sigh.

Wilkie nodded. "A couple more then, and I'll tell you why I want to know. I asked you this already, but again, as far as you know, he didn't spend his money on anything except his Saturday-afternoon outings?"

"He didn't *need* to, mister. He didn't *need* to. I took care of all his meals, and I gave him most of Mr. Maguire's clothes *before* Mr. Maguire died. What else did he need money for? He never complained to me, or asked me for a raise. That wage was fixed between him and my former husband when Thompson first came, and he agreed to it.''

"Actually, I'm interested in the money he had left over, not the money he should have earned. Okay? You say he never got letters. Did he ever ask you for a stamp to send a letter?''

"That would have been more personal than we were.''

"There's hardly any money in his bank account. Where did he cash your checks? It'll say on the back of them.''

"I paid him in cash. That way, we didn't have to bother with deductions and all that.''

"Is that legal?''

"It's not wrong, I know that. That's the way we started out and that's the way we kept up. My bookkeeper in Sweetwater entered it as some kind of contract we had with Norbert. It was up to him to say what he owed the government.''

"Did he spend money on holidays?''

"He used to just take a week off to go to the exhibition in Toronto. But that wouldn't cost him much. He stayed at a rooming house, and he was only interested in the farm animals and such. He never went on no swings or rides or anything like that.''

"Did he keep much in his wallet? I mean, did he like to flash a few bills? A lot of single guys do.''

She stared at him ponderingly, interested now in the question. "No. No, he never made a display of his money. In fact, once or twice I'd need help paying for something at the door—someone selling berries, for instance—but he hardly ever had change of a twenty. He must have kept it somewhere. I never thought of that.'' She looked at Sproat, who nodded, confirming and approving.

''That's what I wanted to know. He might have been the victim of a robbery. If he kept the money by him, like a miser, someone might have got wind of it.''

''Certainly might,'' Sproat said. ''Hear that, Ruth?''

''I hear it,'' Mrs. Sproat said. ''We paid him a lot of money over the years.''

Sproat nodded in half a dozen slow arcs.

''Thing is,'' Wilkie said, ''someone might've figured on a lot more. Someone who knew he didn't keep it at the bank and guessed wrong about his wages, guessed he made the same as other hired men. Someone who could figure that he had maybe twenty thousand stashed away. I mean, how much does the *average* hired man earn?''

But Sproat was equal to the problem. ''Whatever he's worth, mister. That's what Jesus said.''

''You think there's a chance he saved it all up and spent it at the exhibition?'' Wilkie asked, ignoring Sproat.

''I wouldn't think so. He *was* a bit of a miser, like you said.''

''HELP ME THINK, Ernie.'' Wilkie was in Villiers' office again, passing through Larch River on his way back to Sweetwater. ''They paid him a hundred a week.''

''For Christ's sake.''

''Okay, okay. But I'm not concerned with the minimum wage. It seems to me that even on that, there ought to be some money around. Fifty a week for four years.''

Villiers did a sum on a scrap of paper. ''Could be. Want me to find out if he deposited any in Sweetwater?''

''I don't need to rely on you for everything, Ernie, thanks. I already checked that. He had no other bank account than yours, no safe-deposit box, nothing.''

''Better look for a loose brick by the fireplace.''

''What? Oh, yeah. That's what I figure. He had a stash, and someone knew it.'' Wilkie stood up. ''Let me know if someone brings in a sack of money smelling of chicken shit, would you?''

But Villiers didn't smile. He was brooding. ''A hundred a week. Goddam fundamentarians,'' he said.

''I don't know that word.''

''I just made it up. Means religious assholes.''

FIRST, PICKETT STOPPED in at the hardware store and confirmed for himself all that Wilkie had said. He tried to keep the visit at the level of gossip. He didn't want their conversation to be worth remembering in the event that Wilkie should come along after him. Then he asked, ''Did you give the guy good directions to my place?''

''I think so.''

''What time was this? At night, near to closing time?''

''More like the middle of the afternoon.''

''That right? Anyway, what I came in for was a Leatherman. You know it? One of those all-purpose tools. I've lost mine and I'm totally dependent on it.''

The storekeeper shook his head. "Don't carry them. I could order one in."

"I kind of need it today."

"Try Lindsay. You'll find it there."

THE NEXT MORNING, Pickett told Charlotte that one of the floodlights he had bought was cracked and he would have to go back to Toronto for a replacement.

At the Bail-and-Parole Unit, he waited until he could get Marinelli alone. "I'm looking for a guy about thirty, an old hockey player probably, with no upper plate. You know, gummy. Drives a pickup truck."

"On parole?"

"No. Or he wouldn't be driving, would he? You aren't allowed to drive on parole, are you? No, but just maybe he's been around here, possibly on bail." He told Marinelli the rest of the story of the sighting of the hockey player. "He's been inquiring after my cabin," he concluded. "A guy in a pickup truck."

Marinelli held up his hand as Pickett made to continue. "Lemme think." Several long minutes later, he said, "Tell me again. You still think someone's looking for you, someone on our books?"

"I think there's a chance something like that's happening."

"*Is* happening?"

"He's still out there, and he might know now that he made a mistake."

Marinelli asked the obvious question. "If he's around thirty years old and you helped put him away, then it was in the last ten years. No, you worked here for the last six years, and you've been retired for two, so you've only got a couple of years to check to see if you nailed any hockey player. Shouldn't be too difficult.''

Nor was it. Marinelli gave the problem to a young constable who sat down at a computer and began a search, starting with Pickett's name, then scanning the record of convictions for various kinds of homicides, then the list of serious assaults, in the period they had chosen. Pickett recognized three of the names, all of them still in Kingston Penitentiary.

Marinelli responded now like Wilkie. ''I think what you've got is a hockey player looking for a place to build a cabin and trying to get some ideas on how to proceed,'' he said.

''I'd still like to know who he is.''

TWO HOURS LATER, Marinelli looked up in surprise. ''Back again? Still looking for the avenger?''

Instead of driving back to Larch River, satisfied, Pickett had stayed in town long enough to begin to have doubts again.

To Marinelli, he said, ''How about doing me a favor? Ask everyone who has worked here for the last few weeks, every shift, if they can remember anyone passing through who looked like an old hockey player. Or if they know of any old hockey players who've done time.''

''Jesus, Mel, that's a hell of a long shot. Just because a guy with a scar instead of an eyebrow has passed through Shit Creek, or whatever that town of yours is called, about the time your tenant was killed, you can't put out a dragnet for all old hockey players.''

"Why not? Old hockey players known to us, I mean. This guy looked suspicious."

"They all do if they've been in enough fights. On the ice."

"It's suspicious that he was a stranger hanging around the town."

"It's suspicious that he was a stranger. How come the sheriff didn't shoot him on sight? That's the usual way, isn't it, up there on the frontier?"

"Would you do me the favor?"

"Ask all of my guys here?"

"Yeah."

"Christ, Mel—"

"Christ, nothing. Just *ask* them."

Several people looked up, shocked by the raw edge in Pickett's voice as he tried not to shout.

"I'll ask them—" Marinelli became still, quiet, careful, but acknowledging Pickett's concern "—if you'd mind telling me why we should know the guy." He looked around the room to send the eyes away.

Pickett, awkward now, said, "I can't get it out of my skull that it wasn't an accident and that it might have been meant for me. So someone *might* be bearing a grudge. And then there's Charlotte, my wife—"

"Right, right, right. But why us?"

"I've been thinking. Guys who come here to register have to wait in line for a while. This guy *could* have overheard you people talking about me, couldn't he?"

"Ah, come on, Mel. No, right, right, right. I'll ask. Okay?"

"Could you start now, with these guys?"

There was no response from the present shift, so Pickett went home and waited, calling Charlotte to tell her that he was staying over because he wanted his regular service station to give the car a tune-up after their Florida run.

That evening he got a call from Duguid, the sergeant in charge of the evening shift, who had picked up the assignment from Marinelli and received an immediate response from one of the constables manning the desk.

"He said maybe you mean Gruber," he told Pickett.

"Who's Gruber?"

"A guy who fits your description. He was convicted of assault—he beat up a hooker—and had a couple of minor drug charges, and he was a found-in at a booze can we raided. He worked as a bartender for the bikers."

"What address have you got?"

"No address, and I'm kind of busy. Can it keep until tomorrow?"

Pickett swallowed the reply. "Sure. When does Marinelli come back on?"

"Two o'clock tomorrow."

"Leave him a note, would you? Tell him I'll be down to see him about finding Gruber."

"CONNIE GRUBER," Marinelli confirmed. "I don't know where you'll find him, but here's what he looked like the last time we booked him." He handed Pickett two ID shots, side and front.

Pickett started to put them in his wallet.

"What do you plan to do with them?" Marinelli asked.

Pickett had not decided that himself yet. "Take them up to Larch River," he said after a moment. "Try to get an ID."

Marinelli shook his head. "I don't think so. The chance of it being him is kind of remote, and yet you're going to flash his picture all over central Ontario. You should think about that. So should I."

"Why did you guys think of Gruber at all?"

"Because you asked us to. He was in here a few weeks ago."

"Parole?"

"Out on bail, charged with possession. Which he beat with a lawyer the bikers paid for. Now let me ask you a question. Have you ever *heard* of this guy before, let alone been responsible for putting him away? Rack your brains."

"I don't have to. No. But he's been asking around, looking for me. Why?"

"*Someone* his age with scars on his face, a totally respectable minor-league goalie, was around looking for someone to show him how to build a summer cabin and someone told him about your cabin. He wasn't looking for you. Coincidence."

"Let me crop the picture, make it like a real passport photo. No one will know where I got it."

Marinelli laughed. "There's a switch. A prison ID that looks like a passport photo. But I'm still unhappy about it. Suppose you're right? Someone could, just could, report back to Gruber that they are showing his picture around Armpit Landing in connection with a murder, and then this biker/lawyer of his will be down on us like a…biker/lawyer.''

''I won't show it around. I'll show it to only one guy, the kid in the hardware store. If he recognizes Gruber, then I can make up a little story about the license plates on his truck, if Gruber ever gets around to asking.''

''Ask the OPP guy first. Wilkie? That his name? Ask him. Tell him what you're thinking.''

''Sure, I will. No problem. Why?''

''For your own sake. Tell him what you're up to, or you'll be in shit. You know, Mel, you sound obsessed. Just a little.''

''That's what Wilkie thinks, too. I merely want to know if someone's after my hide.''

''Okay.'' Marinelli took the pictures back and cropped them, leaving a tiny head and shoulders on a nearly clueless picture.

''Here.''

''I could have done that.''

''I did it for you.''

''How did you know Wilkie?''

''I don't. You must have told me. Anyway, you tell him.''

''Sure.''

Pickett drove back to Larch River, dropping in on Wilkie on his way through Sweetwater. Once more he just wanted to see if Wilkie had made any progress he could use in his story to Charlotte. He had no intention of bothering the sergeant with his own concerns.

''Just the man,'' Wilkie said, apparently not surprised to see him. "Come up to your cabin, will you? One last look."

"I'll follow you there."

"Make it in an hour. I have to pick up Brendan."

THIRTEEN

"SHE SAYS SHE PAID him a hundred a week. Ten dollars would cover his beer on Saturday, another fifteen at the Chew'n' Chat, say twenty-five altogether. Then his laundry. Five? Another twenty for all the other stuff, the once-a-month haircut, once a year for a new pair of boots, things like that. So he had fifty a week left over. What did he do with it?" Wilkie was talking to his constable, Brendan Copps.

"A woman?" Copps speculated.

"A hooker? Here? What does it cost in Sweetwater? Two hundred would be about right on Jarvis Street, in Toronto."

"We don't have any hookers here. We wouldn't allow it. They would corrupt our youth. No, I meant a girlfriend."

"Did he have one? I haven't heard of one."

"I'll find out."

I wonder how, Wilkie thought. "I still have to think he was targeted for the money someone thought he had. This guy was one of these real rural tight-asses—you know—kept his money in an old milk churn."

"Sounds like my dad," Copps said.

"Yeah? Oh. Well. Sorry. I didn't mean, you know, just—"

"The word you want is 'farmer.' "

"Norbert Thompson wasn't a farmer. Just a hired man."

"He was what we used to call a 'farmer,' when I first came to town. You don't hear it much anymore. Nowadays 'farmer' means the guy who owns a farm. On English television, it means Sir Rupert Doiley, the guy up at the manor house. But here when I was a kid, it meant the guy who kept his hat on in the movies. 'Take your hat off, farmer,' we used to shout from the back row, trying to be the first to shout it. Most of them were called 'Elmer.' You know, 'Don't eat that, Elmer.' "

"What are you talking about?"

"Acting dumb. Like a farmer. The whole sentence is said by the farmer to his kid. 'Don't eat that, Elmer. That's horseshit.' Means don't swallow everything you hear. I'm surprised you haven't come across the expression before."

"I was carefully raised. But you guys, the ones who lived in downtown South Porcupine, you knew better, right?"

"We were cool."

"*You* were. Smokey Stover wound up in jail."

"Yeah. That was the chance you took. But farmers didn't take chances. They didn't have to. Like you said, tight-assed."

"So what happened to you? Your dad was a farmer, I mean a real farmer. Why aren't you?"

"I lived in a boarding house in town through high school. It was the only way. I couldn't commute seventy-five miles over dirt roads twice a day. So I fell in with the townies, and when I finished high school, there was no way I was going back to that quarter-section of dirt we lived on. So I went down to Toronto, worked for a year, then enrolled in the university.''

''What did you take?''

''Engineering. That's what everybody like me took. Or agriculture. But I only lasted one semester. In engineering, I was back with the farmers I'd been trying to get away from. So I tried to transfer. I fancied law, but I didn't have the prerequisites, so I thought maybe if not 'law,' then maybe 'order.' So I became the man you see in front of you.''

''You going to stay with it?''

''Oh, yeah. This is it. I've finally found a role model. You. I wanna be like you.'' Copps burst out laughing. ''Seriously, I like it. It suits me. I can understand you being disappointed after the big city—where did you live? Scarborough?—but I'm at home anywhere. Except Toronto. Anybody I marry will know what to expect. I'll tell her.''

''That's smart. Mine didn't. Know what to expect, I mean.'' Helen had called, making the preliminary noises to prepare the ground to let him know she would not be coming home next weekend. It was the first time she had been away for two weekends in a row.

''I don't think you did, either, Chief, when you transferred from the Metro force.''

There was nothing to be said to this. It was a truth he ought not to have allowed Copps the intimacy to express. ''Can we get back to Thompson?'' he asked.

''Right. You were figuring Thompson was what we used to call a farmer.''

"I just wondered if he understood how the system works. Mrs. Sproat says they paid him a hundred a week and his board. They were screwing him, but I don't know if they knew it or if he did, so *were* they screwing him in fact? Any way I figure, there's fifty a week not quite accounted for—over the years, maybe five thousand? I thought he might have put it in a deposit box, but there's no record, here or in Lindsay, and he wouldn't have gone any farther. Remember, he didn't have any transportation except on Saturdays, and the word is that he spent Saturday afternoons in the beer parlor."

"What about the widow?" Copps grinned.

"Who?"

"The widow. You know."

"No. Tell me about the widow."

"I heard about her from my bachelor great-uncles. Three of them there were, all came over from Ireland together. My grandad was the fourth, and he was the only one got married. When my dad got into the sauce with his cronies, when the wives weren't around, he used to joke about the widow. Once you were sixteen, you were allowed to hear the stories. These three great-uncles, my dad's uncles, farmed the same acreage a little south of Peterborough, and they had sent back to Ireland for their sister to keep house for them. Every Saturday afternoon they would go into Peterborough to see the widow. Separately. I think each one had his own hour to visit."

"She was the town whore?"

Copps screwed up his face in an expression that suggested he was suddenly up to his waist in sewage. "You city people don't understand the subtle nuances of rural culture. There weren't any whores in Peterborough then, still aren't officially as far as that goes, not real Jarvis streetwalkers. No, she wasn't the town whore, or even the town bicycle. She was just a poor widow woman who accommodated my great-uncles. Once a week. They didn't believe she accommodated anyone else, or they might not have carried on. Seriously."

"But they *did* pay her. For a tumble. Right? Don't let me misunderstand these nuances."

"You have, in a way. No. The way the story came down to me from overhearing my dad and his neighbors after a barn raising or some such when they'd had a few, was that they didn't pay her in money. They helped her out, a poor widow lady. One uncle would take her a box of apples, another a sack of onions and a bag of potatoes, the third one half a pig and a couple of roasting chickens. They made sure she didn't go short. Later on, when they got older, they used to go together sometimes, still taking her stuff, all three of them together on a Saturday afternoon to play euchre, and she would cook up the bacon and eggs they brought, and bake a pie, so their sister, my great-aunt, could have the night off."

"Where did the sister go? You making this up?"

"I'm telling you it exactly as it came down to me. There used to be a social at the Catholic hall on Saturday nights. The sister helped out with the refreshments. Her brothers would turn up later."

"Didn't she know where they'd been?"

"She didn't make a fuss. See, the widow was Anglican, so that didn't count."

"You mean on these Saturday afternoons when

they went together, they took turns? Sounds like a whorehouse to me.''

''What dirty minds you Protestants have. No, that wouldn't have been nice. No, what I'm saying is, later on, the three of them turned up together to show the neighbors that they had always been just good friends to the widow, and show her, too, that they appreciated her not just for the nookie. By then, they'd given up the other altogether and just wanted bacon and eggs and a game of cards.''

''So you figure Thompson might have had a widow in Sweetwater?'' Wilkie tried for a tone of skeptical amusement just in case Copps was bullshitting him, but it was very interesting.

''It's possible, but not likely, not these days. It would be hard to find a widow in that sense, these days. The conditions have all changed. It's a lot easier to get your ashes hauled now than it was for my great-uncles, even in Sweetwater. There isn't the same demand for widows,'' Copps replied with a look of candor that was impenetrable.

''Still, if Norbert Thompson had led a sheltered life, he might have been out of date as far as knowledge of the availability of widows is concerned, don't you think?''

Now Copps grinned. ''Could be. And he was from the Maritimes, too, wasn't he? Maybe they still keep up the old ways. I'll see what I can find out. See if I can find an out-of-date widow.''

''Let's go back up to Larch River first. I've got Mel Pickett waiting for us.''

WITH PICKETT AS GUIDE, they tried for the last time to look at the cabin with the eyes of someone seeking to hide something. The floor offered a decent hiding place, but there were no marks anywhere to show where a board had been pried up. The woodpile had been thoroughly taken apart by Wilkie's crew, and in a very short time, there was nowhere else to look.

"What's your idea, then?" Pickett asked.

Once more Wilkie laid out the simple arithmetic. "He took one week's holiday a year, staying at a boarding house in Toronto, which cost him maybe five hundred, so that leaves as much as a couple of thousand a year for four years. Where is it? He had a few dollars in the bank here, nothing significant."

"You had a chat with Ernie at the bank?"

"I had a chat with Ernie. And Thompson had no safe-deposit box or any other account here or in Sweetwater or Lindsay. He had no living relatives except the brother here. So where is it?"

"How old was he?"

"Fifty maybe."

Pickett nodded. "In his prime. A girlfriend?"

"We wondered. Brendan's going to try to find out. There's no obvious sign of one."

Copps started to speak, but Wilkie cut him off. "So we came to have one last look to see where a slightly eccentric, maybe one-brick-missing, fifty-year-old hired man might have hidden eight thousand in twenties."

"Your boys went over the lot pretty carefully," Pickett said.

"They were looking for other things: the weapon, a place where someone might have hid, something he dropped on his way out, like his wallet." Wilkie smiled. "Today we're looking for a little tin box with a slit in the lid. You know?"

"Good luck."

Copps looked out the window. "What about that trailer over there?"

"I'll do that," Pickett said quickly. "Eliza uses that weekends. I've got a key."

Two hours later, the group re-formed in the cabin and Pickett made coffee.

"Without using a mine detector, I think Brendan and I have been over the ground pretty well," Wilkie said.

"Fucking right," Copps agreed. The two OPP men were wet from the knees down from kicking their way through drifts of sodden leaves and pine needles. "We even took the goddam woodpile apart again."

"There's nothing in the trailer," Pickett said. "There's no room to hide anything there, and anyway, I gave Thompson plenty of warning when Eliza wanted to start using it, so he would have taken everything of his out."

"I've never seen a guy with so little *identity*," Wilkie said. "We've got his birth certificate, his hospital card, his Social Security number, and about thirty dollars in cash. That's it. And he didn't have enough spare clothes to tie up in a red handkerchief to go traveling with. There has to be something more."

"Maybe Mrs. Sproat was lying. Maybe she only paid him fifty a week," Pickett said.

Copps said, "Maybe the money never left the chicken farm. Maybe he kept it all in a hiding place there, but when he went to find it, it was gone. She'd found it first. Maybe she figured she was entitled to it, that the Lord had led her to it, because she'd been overpaying him all these years."

Wilkie said, "I don't think Mrs. Sproat is a liar or a thief, just pious. But I'll keep it in mind."

THE ASSISTANT in the hardware store identified Gruber's picture immediately. "That's Connie Gruber!" he shouted. "Used to play for the Longborough Huskies, before he went out to the Maritimes. He got called up to the National League once for about two weeks when a lot of guys were injured in the play-offs." Then the revelation came. "Hey! That's the guy who was asking after you, or asking about your cabin, the day Norbert was killed. I never recognized him then, but I knew him about ten years ago. Well, not *knew* him, but, you know, knew who he was. The dirtiest player in the league. That's him, sure."

"Why didn't you say so before now?"

"I had to see the picture. You know, it's his *picture* I recognize. I never saw the guy in person before, except on the ice with a helmet on. But I remember the story."

Pickett said, "You mind keeping this to yourself? Just between you and me? See, this guy probably has nothing to do with the one the police are looking for, but you know how mud sticks. I'll let you know what I find out, but just now, not a word, eh? Not even to your helper."

"I don't have a helper. I'll keep my mouth shut, don't worry."

FOURTEEN

BACK HOME IN Larch River, Pickett said, "I have to go into Toronto again for a couple of days. It shouldn't take more than that."

"What shouldn't?" She started to fill the sink with water for the dishes.

"There's a guy I want to look up, but I'm not sure where to find him. I'll have to ask around."

Charlotte burst out laughing. "This the way you talked to your first wife? She must have thought she was living in a movie. *'There's a guy I want to look up...I'll have to ask around.'* What guy? Around where?"

"When Mary asked me, I used to say I was working, and I'd call her. She never inquired further."

"Not working now, though, are you? What *are* you doing?"

"Probably making a horse's ass of myself, but I have to follow something up."

"There you go again. What? Follow what up?"

"Okay. I'll tell you what I'm up to. But just between us, please. I could look very foolish. In the last couple of weeks there's been a guy driving round in a pickup truck asking about the cabin. Says he wants to build one like mine. I've been wondering from the time we came up here if whoever killed Thompson wasn't maybe looking for me.''

''God Almighty. Why? Why would he be looking for you? What movie are we in now?''

''I thought at first it might be someone I had put away. A lot of them go down cursing and threatening the guy who collared them. Most of the time, you just tell them they'll have to wait their turn, but there's always the chance that one of them will take himself seriously and try to carry it through. It never bothered me before, but…''

''Go on. I'm listening.'' She turned her back to him and started in on the dishes.

He put his arms around her from behind, partly out of affection, but also to show her what he was really concerned about. ''If someone came looking for me and found you instead, I might have to start all over again, looking through the husband-wanted ads in the Saturday paper.''

''Dear God, you're serious, aren't you?''

''You're a nice target for a punk trying to square his account with me.''

''Take your hands off. What does your pal in the OPP think?''

Pickett gave up trying to treat the matter lightly. ''Look out the window.''

Charlotte pulled the curtain back, then let it fall into place. ''That car is guarding *us?* You asked for a guard? Oh, my.''

''I didn't ask; I saw him this morning when I went to the store for a paper. You asked me what Wilkie thinks. He says he thinks I'm nuts, but I didn't ask him to post that bodyguard out there. That's his idea.

Come the weekend, he'll probably have someone parked on the river road, keeping an eye on Eliza.''

"Eliza will have the Gupta fellow."

"I'd forgotten about him. I'd better tell Wilkie that Gunga Din is on our side." He picked up his keys. "How are you going to manage without a car?"

"I wondered if you would ever ask. I don't know. I didn't realize I would have to manage without a car. I've always had my own up here."

"We should have brought both cars." He sat down to think.

"Next time, I'll ask about your plans for the day."

An awkward moment, one of several dozen so far; he had not had to consider anyone else for the last five years and was out of the habit. And before that, his first wife didn't drive, so the car had been his, not theirs. Still....

"I forgot all about you," he said. That is what the marriage counselor had said to do. Be honest. Say it right away, rather than have *her* say it three weeks later, harboring a grudge, bringing it out when she was angry. "You never crossed my mind."

"Just the car. You didn't forget I was here, did you?" she said. "You'd've said good-bye?"

He laughed. "I guess. But I have to be careful, don't I?"

"Didn't Mary ask for her own car?"

"She couldn't drive."

"Why didn't you teach her?"

"That would've meant I could never be sure where she was. As long as she couldn't drive, she was tied to me, right? That's the way I like wives—dependent."

"But *couldn't* she learn?"

"She tried a couple of times, probably too late in life for her. Hell, if she could've driven, I could've stayed home Sundays instead of trundling down to Hamilton every Christly week to visit her sister. But maybe I had subconscious motives there, too. I don't know what they would have been, though. Nothing to do with Verna, that's for sure."

"Was this Verna really that bad?"

"Was and is. Ever since we had the fight over Imogen, when she arrived from England and Verna thought her son's inheritance was threatened, I haven't had to deal with her. But before that, Christ! I never knew when she'd be making a social call. Her and that kid of hers. And she never ever failed to warn me that the librarian next door probably had her eye on my money, too. For Verna, that would be only natural. I can't wait to tell her about you."

"I'll make sure I'm out that day."

"So will I. Now, do you really need the car?"

"Of course I need the car. You noticed any buses around? But go, go. I planned to do a little visiting, but I'll call around and have them visit me. In the meantime, I'll start in on seeing what we'll put out in the lawn sale." She turned and put her arms around his neck. "If I have to, I can borrow a car from Harlan, my old boss. He likes to have me in his debt. And just think, if you were thirty years younger and we'd been married for ten years, with all this running back and forth to Toronto, I might get worried about another woman, but I don't have to worry about that do I? Just your—what do you call it?—chauvinism." And then, as he was leaving, she said, "Mel, this running back and forth—I know what you just told me, but it hasn't got anything to do with your son, has it?''

He paused with his hand on the door. ''In what way?''

''In *any* way. I was just thinking, nearly fifty years and you never even asked what he looked like?''

''I told you. I went over there sometimes and met with her.''

''But not with him. Didn't she ever bring him along, in the early days?''

''What are you getting at, Charlotte?''

''I'm not getting at anything. I'm telling you, I think it's weird. You don't even have a picture of him?''

''I had no interest in him.''

''That's what's weird. Still, maybe I'll understand one of these days.''

As he left, she asked, ''What am I supposed to say if anyone asks where you are? That Sergeant Wilkie, for instance.''

Pickett went back to the sink. ''Don't tell him, okay?'' He thought about it. ''Tell him I've gone to meet my son.''

He wondered how long it would be before he had a choice of telling Charlotte the truth about his son or letting her decide on a sinister explanation for all this nonsense she was hearing.

IN TORONTO, Pickett threw away the accumulation of junk mail and called on the neighbor who kept an eye on his house to tell her he would be staying the night, and to ask her if she had seen any pickup trucks parked in the street near the house. She had seen nothing. Then he drove down to see Marinelli. He wanted to find out if Gruber was "known," not just to the Bail-and-Parole Unit, and he needed a friend to do the asking. He could think of several people in the College Street headquarters who might help, including Staff Inspector Charlie Salter, whose wife used to invite Pickett to dinner a couple of times a year out of pity for his single status, but all of them would wonder what he was up to and probably suggest he stop it.

Marinelli, oddly, seemed to have no criticism at all. "If we know him, you want to know what he's doing? If he's been seen around? Who he hangs out with?"

"Maybe he's turned respectable. Then I'll relax."

Marinelli put Pickett's request into the pipeline and promised to call him when a response came in.

Pickett said, "I have to get my hair cut and grab a sandwich. Can I call you in a couple of hours?"

"You could try."

WHEN PICKETT called back in the middle of the afternoon, a response had already come in. One of the undercover people on the drug squad knew Gruber, had "bought" small quantities of drugs from him, a tiny amount that would be hard to use as evidence that Gruber was a dealer. He was almost certainly not an important figure in the drug scene, if he was a part of it at all, but he was a hanger-on of a group that drank at the Stairway Tavern on Queen Street, a group that included a leading wholesaler who liked to relax at the tavern when he was clean. The squad had been watching the dealer for months, trying to locate his source of supply. They were fairly sure where and how he distributed the stuff to the retailers, and soon, if they could not get to his source, they would drop on him when they knew he was loaded. Gruber had never been seen in the company of the dealer outside the tavern.

Pickett said, "Drug squad? That's fast. Used to take a couple of days to even make contact with one of those guys. I always used to suspect that when they said they went underground, they meant the subway out to the racetrack. You had to wait until they came home and picked up their messages. No, I'm impressed. Who's your source?"

Marinelli said, "Sergeant O'Dowd."

"I don't know him. But I can't see much connection between building a cabin and pushing drugs, can you?"

"None at all."

"Which probably means that I can forget about him, leave him to the drug squad."

"I would say so."

"Which is what I'll do."

That was for Marinelli's benefit, really more to allow Marinelli not to worry about him.

Pickett drove across town to meet Sergeant O'Dowd, who apparently remembered him from the old days. O'Dowd repeated what Marinelli had said.

Pickett thanked him, then asked, "Have you let the OPP in Sweetwater know?"

O'Dowd said, "I was just about to. Marinelli asked me to. Guy named Wilkie. You know him?"

"You got a minute?"

O'Dowd sat back from his desk. "You going to tell me a story?"

"Sort of."

Then Pickett told O'Dowd in elaborate detail the whole story of the murder, and of the sighting of someone who was probably Gruber, and of the slight possibility that Gruber and Pickett had been connected in the past. His purpose was to place himself in O'Dowd's mind as Wilkie's unofficial right-hand man, his chief assistant in the case. He used "we" a lot, even in those parts of the narrative where he had not been present, like the chicken-farm scenes, as he implied that he was inquiring of the Bail-and-Parole Unit on behalf of Wilkie.

"So now we may have him," he continued, "but we need to be sure. We don't want to pick him up if he's the wrong guy, so I'm going to take a look at him myself first. If I recognize him I'll call Wilkie, who'll have him pulled in."

"And if you don't?"

"We'll have to find out who his friends are. But that's Wilkie's problem. Thanks for the help. I'll take it now."

"Yeah?" O'Dowd shrugged. He rolled the information slip between his fingers and flipped it near the wastebasket. "Lotsa luck," he said, leaving Pickett fairly sure there would be no immediate call from O'Dowd to Wilkie.

PICKETT EXPLAINED to Charlotte that he would be staying one more night in Toronto, because the old colleague in the police department had the day off and Pickett wanted a favor he could get only from him. He spent the rest of the day buying things he and Charlotte liked that were unavailable in Larch River, like pistachio nuts and Algerian olives. By seven, he had done every errand he could think of and drove over to the tavern far too early, to wait for two hours at a quiet table by the door.

One of the patrons, a derelict, nearly ragged enough for the waiters to throw him out, came by his table holding an unlighted cigarette and motioned, requesting a match. Pickett shook his head, but the man persisted, and as Pickett turned around in his chair, looking for a smoker he could direct him to, the man said, "Gruber just came in. He's sitting by the stage with his back to you," and moved off in a search of a light.

Gruber was obviously waiting for someone, sipping his beer and glancing from time to time around the room, checking the other tables. Pickett rose, circled the room and came up behind him.

"Connie Gruber?" he asked, appearing and sitting opposite Gruber at the same time. "Mel Pickett. I hear you were looking for me."

IT WAS OBVIOUS as soon as you thought of it, but it took Copps a surprisingly long time to get there. As a policeman, and as the recipient of a lot of lovers' confidences, he knew that most people had secrets they wanted to tell you, most of which mattered only to the person involved. Sometimes these secrets became public, even though they were nobody else's business, as when the public learned that the senator had died of a heart attack while making love to his cleaning lady and the truth got out before the version from the Prime Minister's office.

Copps himself was an exception; his girlfriends could never complain that they had been deceived, because he told them all about the others—that is, that the others existed. His secret was that he had no secrets, but his women never stopped trying to find out what they were.

When he started looking for a woman Thompson might have known, he had very few places to search. He touched base with Harlan, who confirmed that as far as Larch River was concerned, Thompson was a solitary celibate and nearly a teetotal bachelor. The assistant in the hardware store described him as a decent-seeming, quiet fellow he had never seen in anybody else's company, nor even stopping to chat on a street corner.

So Thompson's social life, as far as it existed at all, was centered in Sweetwater, and Copps returned to the waiter in the beer parlor Thompson had favored.

"Girlfriend?" the waiter wondered. "I saw no sign of one. He just sat and watched a few innings or whatever was on—" he jerked a thumb at the screen "—and made two bottles of Molson's Blue last all afternoon."

"Hookers?"

"No way." The waiter was noisy and decisive. "The owner would have my job if I served one knowingly."

"But if someone was to ask you?"

"I wouldn't know where to tell him to go. Not in Sweetwater. Closest would be Whitby. Besides,

Thompson didn't look like a man looking for a piece.''

"What does a man looking for a piece look like?"

"More like you." The waiter roared with laughter, then wiped the mirth off his face and resumed his customary air of belligerent self-righteousness.

One last possibility had to be looked at because the manner of Thompson's death was entirely consistent with his being a victim of an assault by someone he had taken home. "You think he could have been gay?" he asked.

The waiter grinned without humor. "A fruit? Nah. More into sheep, I would think. Nah."

Copps left the beer parlor and crossed the street to the restaurant. Except for the Laundromat, it was his only hope. But once more the slate was clean: Thompson ate alone, sometimes looking at the weekly newspaper, sometimes not, and he never bothered the waitress. Copps bought himself a take-out coffee and walked down to the Laundromat wondering what else to do, and why Thompson brought his laundry to Sweetwater in the first place instead of using the Laundromat operated by Harlan in Larch River, and then, when he opened the door and saw the woman look up, he realized that he had found the answer to all his questions. How had he missed it before?

He leaned against the wall at right angles to the counter and pulled back the lid of the coffee. "Hi," he said, nodding. "How are you today?"

Not too strong, nearly harmless, but sending a little message. *Well, well, well,* the message said. *This* is *a nice surprise in a Laundromat. Hello again.*

She leaned forward over the counter, "Fine," she said. "Can I help you?"

He sipped his coffee and smiled. "Remember me? I remember you."

"I do now. You're the policeman who was in before, asking about Norbert."

Norbert. She called him Norbert. Somehow he had missed that before, and now it was almost all he needed to know, with a woman like this, anyway.

"That's right. I just wanted to pick up where we left off. I've talked to a lot of people since I saw you last. He was a nice guy, they say. You've got good taste."

She colored, and her hands went up to protect her bosom.

Copps ignored the sign of her fear. "He was lucky to find you. How did you get together? I mean, he was very shy, they say..." He paused, watching the expression of doubt and worry cross her face as she wondered if she had revealed too much to him the last time they spoke. Then she nodded. "Yes, he was. For a grown man, he was. Very shy."

"You are, too. Did it take a long time to trust him?"

Again he watched her perplexity as she tried to decide if she was becoming too confidential with Copps. Cautiously, she answered, "Not so long. I knew he was okay from the beginning."

"Were you kind of...engaged?"

It took a long pause, then she reddened, her secret out, but proud of it. "Kind of. We were going to be married."

"Yeah? When did you get together? No one around here knew he had a girlfriend."

She straightened up. "I don't think that's your business. Why're you asking?"

This had taken so long to come that he was completely ready for it. "Jealousy," he said. "And money. We think about motives, see. Jealousy and money are the two big reasons why people kill each other. He didn't have any money, so I figure it must have been jealousy. Somebody was jealous of him, or maybe of you. You, probably. Someone didn't like you seeing him. Someone from around here, because that's the only place you could ever have been seen together, right?"

"We were *never* seen together."

"Huh? How did that work?"

"We were *never seen* together."

"Never is a big word. How'd you manage that?"

"We got together after I closed this place. Seven o'clock Saturday nights. The Laundromat was still open, but I closed the counter."

"Where did you go then?"

"Upstairs. He took my keys and let himself in the back door and I met him upstairs."

"What's up there?"

"My apartment."

"That right? How long did he stay? I mean, what time did he leave? I'm wondering who could have seen him."

"I don't know why anyone would connect him with me. There're four apartments up there, and three other stores in the block. He could've been coming from any of them."

"Why did you have to be so careful?"

"He wanted it that way. On account of the people he worked for, I think. So did I."

"Somebody guessed, though. Somebody killed him. I mean, we know he didn't have any money. So what else could it be?"

"He had money."

"What?" Copps affected a small surprise.

"He had money."

"How do you mean? A lot of money? In the bank?"

"It was in the bank, but not in his name. I've been listening to you, what you've been saying. Nobody was jealous of either of us, me or Norbert. I never let anyone take a shine to me in Sweetwater before. I don't know about Norbert, but I'm sure there was nothing to be jealous about. I was the only lady he was ever with here. That I know. So it must have been the money. Someone figured out he had a lot of money saved and killed him to get it." She shuddered now, her misery surfacing; her mouth opened and a single quiet wail came out as she turned her head away.

Copps was not sorry to see her misery. Until this moment, she had been too composed for someone whose lover had been recently murdered, suggesting that her emotional world might be awry. Now, though, for Copps, her wretchedness put her back in the world of ordinary people, people with reactions you could understand. A little eccentric perhaps, and certainly not one of his types, but more normal than not.

"Hey," he said gently. "Hey, hey. How'd it be if

we went over there for a cup of coffee? Close up now. Let's go over there.'' He pointed to the restaurant across the street.

She sniffled, nodding. ''We could go up to my apartment,'' she offered. ''Have a beer.''

''Let's go to the Chat'n'Chew.''

''It's the Chew'n'Chat,'' she said, trying for a smile. ''Lot of people get it wrong.''

''Whatever. Let's go over and have a little of each.''

FIFTEEN

"At first we just talked," she said. "You know, we had a cup of coffee before he drove back to the farm. It went on from there."

They were sitting in Wilkie's office with the door closed—Wilkie, Copps, and Linda Perry, the Laundromat operator. Copps sat close to her, across the desk from Wilkie.

"What do you want to know?" she asked, looking back and forth between the two men.

Wilkie opened his mouth, but Copps spoke first. "Tell us the whole story, Linda. What happened the first time? Why did you go up to your place the first time?"

Wilkie stood up and walked to the window.

"We were talking one Saturday night. He came in every Saturday, and I'd got used to him by then, and started to look forward to him coming in. That was about the time I offered to iron his shirts, save him a few dollars."

"How long ago was this?" Copps asked.

"Two years. A bit more. I had come to Sweetwater only a few weeks before that, when I heard about the job. It was so nice to have something steady, and my own place to stay in. I was a waitress in Lindsay and

She nodded. "When Norbert's brother died, we figured to get married and move to the farm."

"Kick out Mrs. Maguire?"

"No, she could stay. Half the farm belonged to her."

"Only half?"

"Norbert's brother told him that because of all the time he'd put in, looking after the farm and him, too, he was leaving half the farm to Norbert. We were waiting for that. But there wasn't any will. So all we had was the money I'd saved, the money from Norbert."

"Did he know about it from the beginning?"

"Not right at first. But after I told him, he thought it was cute, called it a dowry, which is what it could have been. But he still insisted on giving it to me every week. He called it a joint account, but it was just in my name."

Copps stepped quickly to the door to speak to someone outside, and to get himself a drink of water. When he returned and had composed himself, he said, "When Norbert left the farm and moved into the cabin in Larch River, why didn't you 'walk out' together?"

"I wanted to, but he said he'd been advised to keep our relationship quiet for a while, something to do with his rights. So we carried on as before."

"The idea was that you and he would run the farm now. But he didn't know about Mrs. Maguire's boyfriend, did he?"

"He had no idea. It was a real shock."

Wilkie and Copps exchanged signals, and Copps took Linda's hand, patting it. "I think that's all we need, Linda. You've been very cooperative. Mind if I say something? I think Norbert Thompson was a very lucky guy.''

''He's dead now, though, isn't he? But I wasn't doing anything wrong, was I? Not these days. And I didn't *keep* the money.''

''You made the guy happy. Gave him something to look forward to. I mean all the plans you must have talked about. He's gone, sure, but a lot of people never get what you two had.''

There was another smile. ''He was a nice man. So what about the money? I reckon I should still get half, don't you?''

''The money's yours. All of it. Keep it. There's just three of us here who know about it, and two of us think the money belongs to you. Okay? It's your money.''

''Okay, then. If you think so. After all, Mrs. Maguire wasn't very good to him, was she? I was. We was a good pair.'' She stood up.

''Where are you going?''

''Back to work.'' She opened the bankbook. ''I could maybe buy the Laundromat.''

''Take your time.''

Wilkie turned now. ''Who was it advised Norbert about not being seen with you, after he left the farm?''

''A lawyer.''

''Here, in Sweetwater?''

''I think so. Yes, I'm sure. Norbert saw him on Saturday mornings a couple of times. I don't know his name.''

''Thanks, Linda. You've been a lot of help.''

When she had gone, Wilkie said, "I thought she'd be grieving. Crying."

Copps said, "She was crying in the Laundromat. She's kind of excited. She's a little bit unstable, on a roller coaster. She could lose it completely. I'll keep an eye on her."

"Be careful. She could transfer—is that the right word?—over to you pretty easy, you keep stroking her like that."

Copps said, "That's a shitty thing to say, you know that? I just wanted her to feel good about herself. She's had a fuck of a life except for this little bit of time with Thompson."

"Sorry. What do you think Thompson was up to?"

Copps said, "At first, he found himself a fifty-dollar woman. Then it's hard to say what happened, because we weren't there. Could have been the way she sees it, that he thought it was cute to keep giving her fifty dollars to save up for their wedding."

"Or?"

"Or he was being smart, or he got some advice to make sure she didn't have a claim on him."

"That's what I wondered. Kind of ugly, isn't it? But why else would he have been advised to keep Linda out of sight after Maguire died?"

"I can think of two or three reasons. My guess would be that the lawyer anticipated that one day it would be important to establish Norbert Thompson's good character, as they say."

Wilkie nodded. "Villiers told me that Thompson had been asking about lawyers. Time I followed that up, don't you think?"

IN THE FIRST two seconds, Pickett wondered if he had failed to find his target. Gruber's face assumed a look of aggressive outrage as he planned to deny whatever Pickett wanted him for.

"Connie Gruber?" Pickett repeated.

"Who wants to know?"

"Don't you know?"

"No, I don't fucking know. Some asshole comes up, tells me a name. How do I know who he is?"

"You know who *you* are?"

"Fucking right."

"Connie Gruber."

"Fucking right. So?"

"And you know who I am?"

"I told you. No. Yes. You stink like a cop, that's for sure."

"That's right. Sometimes I live in a cabin up in Larch River, but right now I'm assisting the OPP in their inquiries into the discovery of a body that was found in that cabin. The body of a man. Murdered."

Now he had scored a hit. "So?" Gruber said. "Who gives a fuck? I mean, where's Larch River? What are you talking about?"

Pickett waited for Gruber to sort his head out. "You remember Larch River," he said. "North of Lindsay. You were up there last weekend."

Now he watched Gruber decide on the minimum he had better admit, and how he could blend it into his response. "Oh, right," Gruber said. "I was driving around last weekend, sure. I'm looking to build a cottage up around Sweetwater. Larch River? I don't remember. I could've gone through it. Small town? Near a lake? Yeah. I think I passed through it."

"Guy was murdered in my cabin last weekend there. You've been identified in the area."

"I *said* I was there. But I don't kill people, mister. Ask your pals."

"I will. There's always a first time, though. For a drug dealer and a biker bumboy with a record."

"That's it, eh? Pin it on any poor fucker with a record."

"If he's found in the area, he has to say why, doesn't he? You know the rules."

"I told you, I was looking for a cabin."

"A cottage, you said."

"Cottage, cabin, what's the difference? Listen, are you arresting me?"

"I don't have the jurisdiction. It's the OPP who'll want to answer that one. No, I'm not arresting you. But I *am* going to tell the OPP where to find you. They have to be curious about what a character like you was doing in Larch River the night a guy is killed in a cabin, don't they?"

"You playing some kind of game?"

"I'm serious. A guy was killed in my cabin. I'd like to help find out who did it, sort of purge the cabin."

"So what next?"

"What I do now is call the OPP in Sweetwater, now you've told me you were up there, and they'll come and find you. Where are you staying?"

"Fuck off."

"Don't be an asshole. If they want you, they'll find you in ten minutes. But there's something I don't get about you and me and this. Did I ever collar you?"

"Not in my recollection."

"Nor in mine. So there's a story here. Want to tell me?"

"There's no story. I went up north to look for a place to build a cabin."

"Why Larch River? It isn't very pretty, is it?"

Pickett wanted Gruber to say that he had overheard the people in the Bail-and-Parole Unit mention it, maybe overheard them kidding around about how their old colleague, a guy named Pickett, had built a cabin up there, and so, hearing about Pickett's cabin, he had driven up there to look. That would have been okay. That was the story he wanted to believe. But Gruber wasn't saying that, so there was a worry about a little gap that wasn't accounted for.

"I told you, for fuck's sake," Gruber protested.

"Sorry, Connie. It's too big a coincidence. They have to check it out. And you. Tick you off their list."

"What do you mean, check it out?"

Now Pickett concluded an idea he had been playing with ever since he had had Gruber pointed out to him by the undercover man. A small gamble, based on the feeling he had that Gruber had come to Larch River looking for him and could have thought he had found him when he found Norbert Thompson; but there was no reason in the world for Gruber to kill Pickett/ Thompson; you had to know why Gruber had gone to Larch River in the first place.

Could Gruber have heard that Pickett was rich? Had gossip he'd overheard in the lineup in the Bail-and-Parole Unit turned Charlotte into a rich widow whom Pickett had married? Even if that were the case, only an inexperienced fool would set out to assault a former policeman for his money, and while

Gruber was obviously as stupid as most thugs of his type, he wasn't a fool in the street sense, and he wasn't totally new to crime. He would avoid all cops, active or retired.

Therefore, Pickett decided to throw a little reassurance at Gruber, get him to relax while they found out what he was up to. If Gruber decided to leave town now, it might be hard to trail him, even though Pickett had assured him they would. At the same time, he couldn't literally hold him at this point without some help, and he could not involve the undercover man. Catching Gruber would have to wait for tomorrow. Of course he ought not to have come this far without telling Wilkie, but he had thought he would recognize Gruber, see the connection between them, and call for help. Now he would have to tickle him until they had the net ready.

He said, "The most helpful you could be is if you'd take yourself up to Sweetwater tomorrow morning, to the OPP there, see Sergeant Wilkie. Explain what you were doing in the area, so he can cross you off his list."

"Fuck that. Let Sergeant Wilkie come to me. He's the one who wants to talk."

"He's got a lot on his plate."

What Pickett had seen described in fiction as "a look of low cunning" crossed Gruber's features. "Okay," he said. "I'll go up there. I mean, if I build a cabin up there, I'll have to live with those guys, won't I?"

Gruber was an urban rat with a pickup truck and an occasional pocketful of money from a drug deal. To the eye of a purist who had built a log cabin,

Gruber lacked the smarts, the resources, the manual skills, or the sheer stick-to-itiveness to build anything larger than a dog kennel, but Pickett nodded encouragingly.

"They police Larch River, sure. You should cooperate, if you can." He added, "If not, I'll call Sergeant Wilkie. He may ask us to pick you up and hold onto you until he can get in. Depends."

"On *what!*"

"On whatever he thinks connects you with that body."

"*Nothing. Nothing* connects me with any fucking body. *Nothing.*"

"Then there's nothing for you to worry about."

Gruber chewed the inside of his cheek. "How come you know I was up there?"

Pickett shrugged. "I just got a request to check you out. I don't know where they picked up your name. You're known to us, of course."

"Was I seen?"

"I imagine so. Somebody recognized you. You used to play hockey, right? Semi-pro?"

"I was a fucking *pro,* mister."

"So your face was on TV?"

"A few times when I was in the NHL. They don't show the American League in Toronto."

"You know how it is, though. You must have played against hundreds of guys on your way up. Somebody you were with on the Brandon Wheat Kings third line once? Or the Flin Flon Flyers? The Longborough Huskies maybe? Something like that?" Again he watched Gruber considering. If the police really connected him, then they wouldn't leave him loose, even for a night. "If you wanted to hide, you'd need a face-lift," he said. He tapped the idea into place. "Maybe they just picked up your license plates. You know, the highway patrol is taking pictures all the time to catch speeders. So they've got a bunch of numbers recorded as seen close to Larch River the night the guy was killed. They pass them through the computer and there you are."

"I wasn't driving my own truck. I don't own a truck."

"That right? So someone must have recognized you."

"It was while I was driving around that area, looking for a site, that I heard about you, a retired cop, who had built his own place. But I never went near it."

"But they remembered you asking about it."

Gruber said, "When did they find the guy? The dead guy."

"That I don't know."

Gruber nodded slowly, like a man coming to a decision. "Okay. Sure. I'm kinda busy, but I'll go up."

"Tomorrow morning. I'll call and tell them to expect you."

Gruber stood up. "You tell them," he said.

Pickett waited until Gruber had scuttled through the door, then caught the eye of the undercover man, finished his beer, and walked out to the street.

Passing behind him, a few moments later, the undercover man said, "The A & P," and Pickett followed him at a distance into the supermarket and picked up a basket, remembering that the store sold several staples of his former widower diet that deserved to be brought into his marriage, the most important being Patak's vegetable curry. You only had to heat it, shovel it over some rice, add a dollop of Major Grey's chutney, heat two poppodums in the microwave, slice some cucumber into a dish of yogurt, and you had a dinner fit for a rajah. Pickett found the curry on the shelves, chose the medium level of hotness, the can with the blue background, and someone said, "That's pretty hot, ain't it?"

They only had a minute. The months of carefully building his cover could be wasted if the wrong person saw that the undercover man was talking to a cop; Pickett had to concede, after his talk with Gruber, that the whole fraternity could identify him as an old copper.

"You know Gruber?" the man asked.

"He's part of the scene I'm watching. Just a small part. He's nothing, really."

Pickett took down the mild version of the curry and showed him the label. "You know where he lives?"

"Easy to find out. He leaves the bar pissed most nights. Easy to follow."

"Good enough."

"How about the one with the black label? Hot, it says. They mean that?"

Pickett scanned the shelves for a black label until he saw what the undercover man was talking about. Ten feet away, a man in a black bomber jacket was sliding toward them, his ears perked.

"It's real good for a hangover," Pickett said. "As good as chili."

The undercover man nodded, picked up the can and walked to the checkout.

The man in the jacket said, "You know about this stuff?"

"What?"

"Curry. I've had a couple of Indian dinners lately. The first was nice, but the other one took the skin off my tongue. I still like it, though, and I'd like to make my own. I asked the clerks, but I think they're all Ukrainian. They don't know Indian from nothing. Then I heard you guys comparing notes. So, do you mind? Is this stuff easy to make?"

"It's already cooked. All you have to do is heat it. Start with the mild."

"Yeah? And kind of work up?"

"That's it." Pickett walked away, saying over his shoulder, "One can is big enough for two people, three if you're careful."

Outside, the undercover man had gone.

SIXTEEN

PICKETT CALLED Wilkie from Toronto the next morning to let him know what to expect.

Wilkie said, "This is one giant step too far, Mel. If he doesn't turn up, they'll have my ass for letting you near the case. You know that. Deep shit. And I will off-load as much of it as I can on you."

"Gruber will turn up."

"He'd better. I tell you, if it wasn't for the fact that I think this whole Gruber thing is a waste of time—yours, thank Christ—I'd be very, very pissed off. Even more than I am. I'm not as goddam stupid as you seem to think. But there've been a few developments up here, and by the time you get here, I don't think anyone will be worrying about Gruber."

"Like what? What developments?"

"We've got a couple of people here helping the police with their inquiries. I'll fill you in. Then we'll have a serious chat about what retirement means. Okay? Right now, I have to talk to a lawyer."

WILKIE WAS STILL keeping an open mind because it was still a possibility that someone, reasoning as he did before the talk with Linda Perry, had been looking for the treasure that an old bachelor might keep under the mattress. But the discovery that Norbert Thomp-

son was a disappointed man led to some new specu-
lation. First things first. First he had to find the lawyer
that Thompson had consulted.

It might have taken twenty phone calls, but Wilkie
made it on the seventh. He identified himself and
asked the lawyer if a Norbert Thompson had consulted him recently.

"If you mean the man found dead in Larch River,
yes. He was my client."

"What did you do for him? There's a sum of
money that—" Wilkie had intended making a refer-
ence to the missing part of Thompson's wages, but
the lawyer cut him off.

"Advice, for which I charged him three hundred
dollars. That the sum of money?"

"There's no receipt that we can find."

"Then how did you get onto me?"

"Police work." Wilkie realized that he had just
caught this lawyer out in some probably tiny breach
of the law, like pocketing a cash fee and planning not
to declare it in his income-tax return.

"Did you issue a receipt?"

"Not yet."

"When did you give this advice?"

"A few weeks ago."

"January?"

"It might have been."

"Are you free? Now? I'd like to come over there
now."

"I could free myself."

"I'll be right down."

BYRON TOOGOOD, barrister and solicitor, had a law
office in the municipal building, a small, concrete-

block structure that housed the local government offices, the elected officials, including the mayor, and a number of commercial tenants on the second floor, including Toogood. He was a handsome man in his midforties who groomed himself carefully. He was obviously fit—squash probably, Wilkie thought; there was a club in Lindsay. His clothes, though they looked casual for the working dress of a small-town lawyer—leather jacket, collarless shirt, boots—looked faintly like the costume of an actor playing the part of Byron Toogood. The lawyer and his outfit were out of place in Sweetwater, and Toogood gave off an air of being slightly contemptuous of his world.

"What did Thompson pay you to advise him about?" Wilkie asked, keeping the clouded payment fresh in the conversation.

"My practice is primarily in family law—" Toogood began.

"What does that mean?"

"Most of the time, representing one of the parties in a dispute."

"Like divorce?"

"That's part of it."

"Thompson was a bachelor. What's the other part?"

"Property rights, wills."

"Thompson wasn't his brother's heir as long as Mrs. Maguire was alive, so where did you come in?"

"You know the situation at the farm, before the brother died?"

"Norbert Thompson was the hired man."

"Making a hundred a week."

"And?"

"Board and room, of course."

"I meant 'And?' like 'So?' You seem to find that remarkable."

"A hundred a *week?*"

"He saved a little, though, didn't he? Three hundred for you, for instance."

"The final bill would have been a lot bigger. I billed him just for the initial meeting. He'd been in several times since then."

Now Wilkie got a glimpse of light. "Were you working for him on a contingency basis?"

Toogood shook his head. "Not as such, no. But I expected to be paid eventually."

"So if I find he had a few hundred dollars stashed away, will you make a claim on it?"

"It's too much trouble now."

"What were you advising him about?"

"His rights. I thought he had a claim on the estate by virtue of what he did, how they interrelated, what he was promised."

Wilkie sat back. "Tell me. The man's dead. You mean he wasn't the hired man?"

"You remember, a few years ago, somewhere in the Maritimes, a case of a woman living common-law with a farmer, and they split up? She claimed a portion of the farm on the grounds that she had been his partner as well as his wife—marital duties, including running the house and helping out with the farm. She won."

"Was the sex important?"

"She had to establish that she had been the same

as a wife, because it was already established that a divorcing wife would be entitled. So it was helpful.''

"Apply this to Norbert Thompson. I think I can do it myself, but go ahead anyway."

"As I understand the terms, women-persons are the same as men-persons. Right? And when a woman-person and a man-person separate, each is entitled to half of what they have jointly accumulated. It's more complicated than that, but that's the basic idea. So if Thompson had been a woman kicked out by her male companion, she would have had every feminist in Ontario campaigning for her. No, she wouldn't have needed them, because nowadays it's automatic."

"So you took the case. On a contingency basis."

"I didn't worry about the money; I just thought it would be a good case to win."

"So what did you advise him?"

"That he had a case."

"But she paid him a hundred a week."

"A lot depends on what you think that means. It looks to me like they took advantage of him. The guy did everything. They fed him and gave him pocket money, and one day off a week. For that, he ran the farm."

"And he did a husband's duties with the sister-in-law, as they say in the Bible?"

"Well, no, he wouldn't allow that. He didn't even want to talk about it. No, what he was sure of was the promise made him by his brother, who told him he'd left him half the farm in his will, and he hoped Norbert would continue to look after his wife. In fact, he made Norbert promise to marry his wife when he was gone. It was a secret, though. Mrs. Maguire herself wouldn't hear of any such talk. But he couldn't have lived with her at the farm unless he did marry her, could he?''

"You know that Mrs. Maguire got married again right away? To someone else. What do you make of that?''

"I think Norbert Thompson got screwed.''

"Do you think Maguire, the sick man, knew that Sproat was in the wings, that sort of thing?''

"I wouldn't think so.''

"Do you think Norbert Thompson knew about Sproat?''

"I doubt it.''

"And you advised him to sue?''

"We hadn't reached that stage. I went over the ground, told him his rights.''

"As you saw them.''

"As a judge might see them.''

"You never met with him again? Why not? Didn't he want you to represent him?''

"I believe he wanted to try it on his own first.''

"Ah. So he went to see Mrs. Sproat, as she was now known as?''

"I understood that he was going to.''

"But you never saw him again to find out what happened.''

"No.''

"I'll have to ask Mrs. Sproat that, won't I? Tell me, though—what about his rights under Maguire's will? Didn't the will promise him half the farm?''

"So Thompson claimed. But the will hasn't appeared.''

"Did you know that the farm always belonged to Mrs. Sproat?"

"I found it out very quickly. I advised Thompson to forget about that claim, concentrate on his other rights."

"And you did think Thompson had a case?"

"Of course. That's why I was advising him."

"Yeah, but did you *really* think he would win?"

GRUBER HAD NOT appeared at the OPP detachment when Pickett arrived at eleven. They waited for an hour; then he and Wilkie crossed the street to the Fisherman's Wharf, a diner on the main street specializing in pot-roast sandwiches. Over sandwiches and coffee, Pickett gave Wilkie his account of his Toronto adventure.

"I think he heard my name when he was in the lineup at the Bail-and-Parole Unit. I think they were probably making fun of me. You know, 'Old Mel Pickett and his log cabin,' or maybe 'Pickett and his new wife, did you hear?' That sort of stuff. So Gruber heard that a former cop was building a cabin in a place called Larch River."

"So he wanted to build one and he drove up to see how it was done. Like the kid in the hardware store said."

"Then why didn't he say so? Why didn't he say, 'I heard a guy in the B-and-P Unit shooting off about your cabin, so I drove up to have a look. I was hoping you would give me some tips.'"

"You know who you're dealing with, Mel. Guys like Gruber automatically lie to us until someone, a lawyer usually, tells them to tell the truth, or they carry on lying. They do it to give themselves time to think, while they're wondering which of their latest activities we've caught up with. A guy like Gruber is starting to lose track of what's allowed and what isn't. Somebody got killed, and he probably overheard that later, maybe in the same hardware store. People like Gruber have the experience to know we'll take a hard look at someone like him if we find him near a body. I mean, wouldn't we? Aren't you now? Gruber now? I'll give him until—what?—sundown?—isn't that the usual deadline?—before I ask the Toronto people to pick him up.''

"You don't think this is real?''

"Actually, now I think we should talk to him, because where is he? He's taken off. But that's the only reason. In my right mind, I tell myself to forget about him. You sure you're not connected in the past?''

"I've been through his record. We never touched. But I'm goddam sure we're connected now. *I'm* the reason he came up to Larch River.''

"Easy, Mel. You'll frighten the customers in here. I guess trusting him to come up here kind of lets you prove your point, doesn't it? There's no problem. First thing in the morning, I'll send a message down to Toronto to reel him in. He's been identified near the scene of the crime, and we can find out his license-plate number.''

"That won't work. He said it wasn't his truck, and I believe him. Stick to visual ID.''

AND THEN the call came in to headquarters from the owner of The Quiet Man to say he had just repaired the muffler of one Aaron Sproat.

"Let's think about this," Wilkie said. "The lawyer told us that Thompson *might* have called on the Sproats to argue his rights. And Sproat's was one of how many mufflers they repaired this week?"

"Eight," Copps said. "And I've checked out the other seven. None of them looks to have any connection with Thompson or Sproat or a kid joyriding around on Friday night. All good, decent, bingo-playing, grocery-shopping, in-law-visiting folks. Salt of the earth. It's *Sproat* we want to talk to, even if it's just to cross him off the list.

"But there's something else," he went on. "When the muffler man was telling me this, he told me about another pickup truck that came by on Friday morning, asking for directions to Larch River. He'd forgotten about it until we talked a lot about all the pickup trucks with broken mufflers. This one didn't have a broken muffler, and anyway, if it did, the owner could probably fix it himself—it was a welder's truck. A white three-quarter ton. Now, didn't we hear about a welder's white truck around the cabin? So I asked the muffler guy if he could remember what the driver looked like, and it checks out. He'd been in some fights, the guy said. And the other guy looked like a rough customer, he said."

Wilkie said, "I put that truck on the computer, across the province, got everybody looking for it."

"I'll ask Metro again," Copps said. "These guys sound like they belong in Toronto."

SEVENTEEN

THEY HAD NOT had to look long or hard for Gruber. He was found in the emergency ward of the Toronto General Hospital. His head had been kicked several times, and his internal organs were at least heavily bruised by the same boots driven into his stomach. His assailant had been interrupted before he could finish the job.

Wilkie called Pickett with the news. "The way they talked, he's going to be there for a few days, so I can talk to him at any time. The Metro police have put him under guard, just in case someone tries to garrote him a second time."

"When will you go in?"

"I think I'll leave it until he's fit to be moved. Then I'll have him brought up here."

Pickett put down the phone. This time he told Charlotte they wanted him in Toronto for an identification parade.

Charlotte asked, "Is this really the way it was when you were working?"

Pickett said, "This is more interesting. I never actually got to solve any cases during the time I was on the force. Mostly, someone would get killed and the neighbors would sit on the killer until we arrived. Even if he got away, the neighbors would tell us who he was. Either that or we never found the guy. That happened about twice a year. But here I am retired and looking at two genuine mysteries in two years. Amazing, isn't it?''

"You're just chasing fire engines, then?"

"That's it. I'll call you if there's any chance I won't be in for supper. What are we having?"

"Steak-and-kidney pie."

"I'll be here."

THE NURSE SAID, "The patrol from the Indian mission found him unconscious in an alley behind Gerrard, east of Church. They called for an ambulance, and the ambulance brought in the police."

"Has he said anything?"

"Not to us. I don't know if he responded to the police officer. The policeman came back this morning for a while and sat by his bed. I think he's coming again after lunch."

A doctor appeared, wooden clogs clacking down the hall. "No flowers?" he asked. "What kind of friends has he got?"

"Can I talk to him?" Pickett jerked a thumb at the bed.

"Certainly. Ask him whodunit. But he's probably bound by the code of silence." He snickered to show he was joking.

"Will he live?"

"I haven't determined the size or extent of the internal injuries yet, but judging by the fact that he's stopped pissing blood, I think they won't be fatal. According to the X-rays, his head is in one piece, and his neck is bruised by an incompetent attempt to garrote him. Incompetent, but serious. I understand that the would-be executioner was interrupted. So talk to him, tell him all you want is a name, just one name.''

The doctor acted out the last phrases melodramatically, like a character in a gangster movie. Pickett wondered if the doctor had been taking his own medicine.

The doctor continued. ''I'll stay with you for a few minutes, make sure you don't beat him up again. Then I'm going home. I'm too young for this. Hang on, I'll be right back.'' He disappeared from the room in answer to his name being paged along the corridor.

The nurse said, ''He gets a bit silly near the end of his shift, but he doesn't shout at us however tired he is.''

When the intern returned, he leaned over the bed and said, ''Connie, baby. The fuzz is here. He wants to know who fucked you over. Who was it, baby?''

Gruber opened a tiny bright-red eye set in a bed of ripped flesh. The other eye was covered with a dressing. Then he saw Pickett and closed his eye again.

''See?'' the intern said. ''Omerta. They never talk.''

''Ask him again.''

The intern hung over the bed. ''Connie. Name the sonofabitch so we can string him up by his balls.''

Gruber lay unmoving, and now the intern spun around, opened his arms and swept the visitor from the room. ''That's it. Come back in four hours. Let him sleep.''

''I'm going to tell the guard to come in the room and stay with him.''

''Fair enough. But your man is not to sit by the

bed, his ears pressed to the patient's lips, okay? You can probably wait a few years for this guy's last words. Right now, leave him alone until the doctor on the next shift shows up. He's in no danger. He needs rest, like me. Y'all hear that, Nurse?'' he added in a fake Southern accent.

She nodded and closed the door of the room, and the intern clacked along to the elevator, where he did a little dance and sang a bit of the *Largo El Factotum*, apparently to celebrate the end of his shift.

Pickett walked over to the Pickle Barrel for a corned-beef sandwich, killed an hour in the World's Biggest Bookstore, then made his way back to the hospital.

When he appeared at the nurses' station, the nurse on duty paged the resident, who arrived in a few minutes. "What do you want to know?" he asked. "The intern got it right. Someone beat this guy up and tried to strangle him, kill him. Seriously. His stomach is bruised, but the internal organs seem okay. You want to talk to him? Go ahead."

The resident led the way into the room and leaned over the bed. "Mr. Gruber," he said. "A visitor."

Gruber did not open his eye. "Where from?" he asked.

Pickett said, "Remember me, Connie?"

Gruber turned away. Pickett walked to the door with the doctor. "How long can I have?" he asked.

"What are you going to do?"

"Ask him some questions. Usually you guys say 'ten minutes, no more,' something like that. Don't you?"

"That's television. *I* sure as hell don't know how

long is right. I guess if he was nearly dying, I would give you five minutes. But he's all right. Half an hour? He's full of painkiller. He will fall asleep on you before then.''

Pickett returned to the bedside, watched by Gruber. One of Gruber's ears had been bandaged, and there was a line of dried blood under Gruber's lower lip, suggesting he had now lost what few teeth had survived his hockey career.

Pickett said, "Tell me what happened, Connie.''

Gruber was silent, his red-veined eye swiveling back and forth.

Pickett said, "We want to know who clobbered you.''

Gruber shook his head fractionally.

"They found you in an alley with some guy trying to strangle you. Another minute, you'd have been gone. Somebody tried to kill you, Connie. We'll look after him. Who was it?''

Again Gruber shook his head.

Pickett said, "What kind of asshole are you? Guy kicks you in the guts, ruptures your spleen, puts the boots to your face, then tries to garrote you. Would've, if that Indian patrol hadn't come along. And you don't want to tell us who it was?''

"I'll look after him, when I get out.''

He had to lean over the bed to hear the whisper, and not all the syllables came through, but the message was clear enough.

Pickett said, "Great. So now we have to trail you around until you find him? That's bullshit. But then, I'm Metro. This isn't my problem. The OPP is investigating a death in Larch River, remember? I'm here to tell you that as soon as you're okay—okay enough, that is—they're taking you up to Sweetwater and charging you with some kind of homicide. You've been identified as the guy asking after the dead man; you were there when he was killed; and now I think what's happened is that whoever went for you was after your money, the money he thinks you took off the guy in the cabin in Larch River.''

It was impossible to read any reaction on the bruised and scratched face staring up at him, but again Gruber shook his head and said nothing.

''Who was it, Connie?'' Pickett asked. ''We can put him away for seven years just by showing the judge a picture of your face the way it looks right now. You know who it was, don't you?''

Gruber said nothing.

''Maybe you'll talk just before they send you down. Be too late then.''

Gruber said nothing.

Pickett went out to the hall and asked the nurse to call the resident. When he appeared, Pickett asked him when Gruber could travel, in a car.

''Couple of days.''

Pickett said, ''What I want here is total security. No visitors, no calls, no answers to questions. Don't even tell anyone whether he's still here or not.''

''You expecting trouble? This is a hospital.''

''They'll leave the guard on.'' He nodded at the constable. ''No one allowed in except hospital staff you recognize, or someone the nurse at the desk can vouch for. Okay?''

''Those are my orders. I'm supposed to be protecting him. By the way, who are you?'' the constable asked.

"Special Services," Pickett said. "Liaison."

He left the hospital and walked down University Avenue to College Street, to police headquarters. Inside the building, he found the office of the sergeant heading the investigation into Gruber's assault, introduced himself as a "messenger from the OPP" and told him what he knew. He concluded, "You are going to have to be lucky to find the guy. It could have been any of Gruber's close friends."

PICKETT FELT HIMSELF in a bind. Any moment now, if it hadn't happened already, a phone would ring on a desk in Toronto or Sweetwater and Wilkie would learn that Pickett was impersonating an officer, taking the Gruber case much further than he should have. What he should have done was to refer all his doubts to Wilkie in the beginning, and stayed home to look after Charlotte.

But Pickett was having a nightmare. When he was rational, he did not think there were any more than a couple of coincidences: the first, the possibility that Thompson had been mistaken for him, and the second, that a broken-down hockey player turned hooligan was asking for him around Larch River, which was connected with the first. And he also knew that Wilkie was carefully putting together a case involving the Sproats. But Pickett was newly married and he was afraid. He felt strongly the possible threat to which he might have exposed Charlotte, and even Eliza, because they were associated with him. He wanted to eliminate Gruber, whereas Wilkie, so far, had given no sign of regarding Gruber as a serious suspect.

So instead of going home, Pickett called Charlotte to tell her he might be late.

Charlotte said, "You are retired, aren't you?"

"They want me to look at some more pictures."

She sighed. "You know what's for supper?"

"Offal," he said. "I'll be there by eight."

He hung up. He would give Gruber another hour. He sat there musing on "offal," trying to give his anxiety a rest.

He had acquired a taste for kidneys in England, where he had been stationed with the Royal Canadian Air Force at the end of the war. Charlotte was the second Canadian woman he had met in forty years who liked to eat kidneys, as the variety of meats that appeared on the tables of his acquaintances shrank every year. Veal had disappeared; lamb had never been popular among the policing classes; and it was harder and harder to buy many of the old cuts of beef—pot roast, oxtails, tongue—in the supermarkets. Even brisket was going.

"No Offal" the signs in the Bournemouth butcher shops in 1944 proclaimed. And of what the English called offal—liver, heart, kidneys, tripe, and sweet-breads—only liver was easy to find, and no one among his acquaintances ate that anymore. Pickett was the only Canadian he knew who had ever eaten heart; presumably, hearts were ground up for dog food. Soon there would be a choice among steak, hamburgers, or pork chops, with sirloin-tip roast for Sundays. To have gotten two wives who liked kidneys was really something.

ON THE WAY OUT to the chicken farm, Copps asked, "What are we hoping for, Abe? I mean, what do you think we'll find?"

"I think they'll say, 'It's a fair cop,' something like that."

"You think they did it? Or one of them?"

In fact, Wilkie was beginning to have no opinion at all. He had not entirely set aside his original preference for an assault during a robbery, but the connection between Gruber and Pickett was beginning to look as if it would turn into something. Now the news that Sproat had a defective muffler on Friday night offered another line entirely.

"I was taught never to theorize," he said. "Get the facts."

"You can't help guessing, though, can you?"

"So what do *you* guess? Did one of the Sproats clobber him?"

"No."

"What about the muffler?"

"It's not much, is it?"

"Let's hear their story first."

"Okay. When we get there, I'll take a look around the farm."

"Why?"

"Just in case I guessed wrong. I've been thinking."

"About what?"

"I'll tell you after, okay? Just a dumb idea that might fit a very dumb suspect."

ONCE SPROAT had called off his dogs, Copps stayed outside "to get some air," as he put it.

Wilkie sat down with the husband and wife. "Mrs.

Sproat," he began, "I found out something I didn't know when I was here last. I just learned that Norbert Thompson was entitled to half of this farm."

"Who told you that?"

"Point is, is it true?"

"I seem to remember telling you when you first came here that this farm belongs to me, always has. It came down through my great-grandfather, who cleared the land. So there's no way Mr. Maguire could have left Norbert half of it."

"But Thompson believed your husband. He came out here to tell you that, didn't he?"

After a long silence, Mrs. Sproat seemed to take in air, inflating slightly. "He came out here once, yes, and said such things."

"Why?"

"Because he'd been told to, I reckon, by that lawyer. But I spoke to our church lawyer, and he said Norbert had no rights at all."

"Thompson said your husband made promises, is that right?"

"So Norbert said."

"You think he was lying?"

"I don't know what to think. I never thought of Norbert as a deceitful man, but if he wasn't lying, what am I to think about Mr. Maguire?"

Sproat leaned forward. "Mr. Maguire was in great pain, and he wanted to make sure that Norbert Thompson would stay on the farm and look after his wife. So he could've made promises he wouldn't have made otherwise. That's what I think."

Mrs. Sproat waited for Wilkie to respond to this version.

Wilkie asked, "You don't think Thompson had a case? Never mind the lawyer."

She looked troubled, hoping Sproat would speak.

"Tell you the truth, I thought he did," Sproat said. "But not the same one he thought he had."

"We didn't know," Mrs. Sproat said, after several attempts to clear her throat. "I'm sure Mr. Maguire acted for the best."

Sproat put his hand on his wife's arm. "When Thompson came out to make his claim, that was the first I heard about his wages, what they were." He looked at Mrs. Sproat. "It wasn't enough. I told her that."

"It was what was agreed," his wife said. "I'm sure at the time it seemed fair. We didn't know."

"But he *was* underpaid," Sproat said.

"And?" Wilkie prompted, into the silence.

"When he left, I told Mrs. Sproat what I thought, and I said she ought to think about paying him some kind of compensation. Not for not getting half her farm, but for all the back wages he should have had. So I said. I said it was right, and anyway, if it got into court, a hundred a week would sound bad."

Mrs. Sproat nodded.

"So did you?" Wilkie asked.

Mrs. Sproat said, "I wanted to do what was right. I asked the church lawyer, and he said we mustn't offer anything, that it would weaken our position. So we didn't. I wish we had. There was other things, too. I don't want to go into them."

"Was that the last time you saw Thompson, either of you?"

Now she looked at her husband in misery. Sproat

took in a deep breath, but before he could speak, Copps, who had been standing in the doorway for several minutes, brought out from behind his back a piece of two-inch dowelling and held it up.

"I found this in the truck," he said. "Under some sacking."

Mrs. Sproat looked puzzled, then alarmed. "What—" she began.

Sproat put a hand up to stop her. "That's it, I guess," he said. Then, with a formal attitude, he said, "That piece of wood is one I removed from the home of Norbert Thompson, after I struck him with it."

Mrs. Sproat said, "Aaron? You?"

For a moment, Sproat seemed less sure of himself. "Yes. I did it to stop their dirty mouths, and that's all I'll say."

EIGHTEEN

THEY LED HIM out past a paralyzed Mrs. Sproat and took him to Sweetwater to be booked. When he was safely tucked away, Wilkie said to Copps, "You guessed wrong, then."

"Yeah? I still don't think we've got a neat answer."

"Why, for Chrissake?"

"See, that piece of wood was in the wrong truck. It should have been in the one with the new muffler. But it was in the other one. Don't ask me why. We'll find out soon enough."

Wilkie picked up a message from his desk. "When did this come in?"

"Half hour ago," the duty constable said. "There's another one from the Metro force."

Wilkie turned to Copps. "They've found two white three-quarter-ton welding trucks. Only two. I guess it's a silly color for a welding truck. Anyway, one is accounted for, been working for a week welding steam pipe in a factory installation near Burlington. The other one isn't. It's sitting in a driveway of a house on Eastern Avenue. They've checked it out. The owner—the welder, I guess—let a guy named Gruber borrow it last Friday. There was someone else with him, guy named Dougal. They took the truck

Friday morning and brought it back early Saturday morning. Now I have to go into Toronto." He read the second message. "Jesus Christ! I hope I'm in time. Look after Sproat until I get back."

WHEN PICKETT RETURNED to the hospital, Gruber was lying with his head slightly propped, staring at the door, looking as if he was ready to take on all comers.

"I'll talk when I thee a lawyer," Gruber said, revealing that the loss of his remaining teeth had produced a lisp that came oddly from the battered face.

"Fine," Pickett said. "I'll arrange to have you shipped up to Sweetwater this afternoon. I just drove down for a chat, but if you don't want to talk, I'll go back. But that's it. From now on, I'm going to do everything I can to nail you."

Gruber said nothing, waiting for more explanation. He tried to speak, but had to clear his throat, swallowing several times. "What givths?" he asked finally.

Pickett said, "You killed the wrong guy. I'm alive, but the guy you assaulted is dead. The only problem I have is to know why you did it. Not that it matters much."

"I don't know what you're talking about."

"Christ. Listen," Pickett said. "We've got you driving around Larch River on the night a guy was killed. You're identified, you know that, but you're still hanging around like the asshole you are, waiting to be picked up. Why?"

"I'm not thaying nothing."

Pickett said, "I've been thinking while you were passed out. Wanna hear? Here's what I've been thinking, then. I forgot there were two of you in the pickup. But I remember you told me it wasn't your truck. I assumed you'd borrowed it then, but I think now it was *his* truck. He just needed you to drive. So I wondered why would that be? Maybe he didn't have a license. But he had a truck. Maybe his license was void. Probably. Why? Then I realized this guy's on parole; he's surrendered his license, hasn't he? He can't risk being stopped without a license, so he gets you, everybody's stick boy, to take him up there. And you did all the inquiring. He killed Thompson, but no one saw him or knows who he is. How's that?"

"I'm not thaying nothing."

"You admit you were driving around Larch River that night, but it's a coincidence that a man was murdered, you say. Now we've got you, and we know about the other guy, we know why you and he were together, don't we? He needed you to drive him up to Larch River to kill me. Right?"

"I didn't kill anyone."

"I'm inclined to believe you didn't. Otherwise, you would have been very surprised when I caught up with you the other night. You'd have fainted probably, because you'd have known I was a ghost. I mean, if you'd killed him, you'd have known, right? So I think it's likely the other guy killed him. Maybe not. Be patient, Connie. This is all coming clear in a hurry. Maybe you did a run-up, a kind of reconnaissance, for him. Then, thinking the place was empty, you took a look around to see what you could steal, and you found some money, a lot of money. Then you got interrupted by the guy you thought was me and defended yourself, as your lawyer will say, killing the guy in the process.

"The next bit is tricky, but I think something like this happened. Your pal tried to blackmail you. Yeah, he knew about the money and tried to blackmail you. He knows how smart the police are these days, and he knew that you would have left a fingernail or a piece of snot behind, something we could identify you from, so he blackmailed you. Told you he wanted the money or he'd turn you over to us, as is natural with you guys. So you said yes, then you had a think. You saw how you could turn it all around. See, you said to yourself, '*He's* the one with the motive. *He's* the one who wanted Pickett dead.' You were just the driver. That was the way it was supposed to be, wasn't it? So you thought, 'Why don't I tell him to stick his threats up his ass? Better, why don't I blackmail *him?*' Well, maybe not quite blackmail, but something similar.

"So you say to him 'No.' You say, 'Stay away from me or I will turn you in.' Maybe you even go down the road a little, start to act it. 'Why did you kill him?' you say. 'You shouldn't have killed him. I mean, not after you've been blowing all over about how you're going to get Pickett. You should've waited.'

"Then he's stuck. He don't trust this little bastard who's been chauffeuring him around. I mean, how could he? Trust *Gruber?* So he knows that his secret's not safe with you. We're gonna believe you more than him, given a choice, because he's the cop-hater, not you. He's the one we want tucked away for the rest of his life. So he sets you up, finds a way to get you alone in the alley—who helped him, Connie? Some hooker offering a two-dollar blow job? And now he's got you in the alley, and you're about to go under. Then the Indian patrol comes by and that's that, for the time being. You're in the hospital, and he's waiting for you to come home. I told you I didn't understand that bit. But now I just realized he didn't know we'd identified you, you hadn't had time to tell him, or maybe you did but he believed you when you said you hadn't ratted on him. That being the case, there was still time to kill you and keep it that way.

"He didn't think we'd look too hard for whoever did it, because usually if you scumbags can kill each other off, it saves us a lot of trouble. And the public doesn't mind. The headline says that four bikers die in a shoot-out. 'Good,' says my cousin who keeps a pet shop in North York. 'Maybe they'll all kill each other off.' But you're different. You kill civilians. 'Get that guy,' my cousin says. 'He hurts people.' What do you have to say for yourself, Connie?"

"I didn't kill the guy."

"That's *exactly* what *he'll* be saying, Connie. 'I didn't kill him; it was Gruber,' he'll say. I wish I could tell you we don't mind, could share it out between you. Fifteen years apiece. But we do mind, Connie, we *do* mind. You're a punk, a punk with just enough brains to be useful without knowing you're being used—but him, he wanted to kill me. We'd much rather have him than you. So tell us. Who is he?"

"I'm thaying nothing until I thee a lawyer."

"Fair enough," Pickett said. "They're a bit short of space up in Sweetwater, so we're going to have to leave you here for a few days. Next time we meet, you'll be in leg irons.''

Gruber's eye swiveled back and forth between Pickett and the wall while he tried to absorb all he had just heard.

"THAT WAS VERY GOOD, Mel, old son. Like an aria. No, like one of those long bits between the arias when they have to keep singing even though they have no tune.''

Pickett looked up to see Wilkie standing in the doorway, not smiling, and wondered where to go next. He was caught, as he knew he would be, without any exit, involved in a serious breach of the law, not to speak of the personal offense of not telling Wilkie what he was up to. And he had been warned. An enemy could throw some serious charges at Pickett; at the very least, Wilkie would no longer drop by for a chat, but it would probably be more than that, just to cover Wilkie's ass.

Now Pickett said, grabbing at the possibility of lightheartedness behind Wilkie's simile, "I was rapping. You know?''

"That what it was?''

Flinching under Wilkie's scrutiny, Pickett said, "You didn't seem to be taking it seriously, Abe. Have you been listening to me for long? It *is* serious. I have to take it seriously. How did you know I was here?''

Wilkie unbent an inch. "Give me some credit, will you? Give me some fucking credit, for Christ's sake. I'll take it anyway. Just so you'll know, I'll tell you what's been happening on the other side of the mirror, shall I? We don't need an audience, though. Leave this—'' He gestured at the bed. "He isn't going any-where." He turned to the guard. "If he sits up, hand-cuff him to the bed." He turned back to Pickett. "Come down to the cafeteria."

They proceeded in silence to the basement, where they bought coffee and took up their positions.

Wilkie said, "First, a fact of life about us, a fact you seem to have forgotten. I asked my dad. He was amazed that you thought you could get away with conducting your own secret investigation. Thought you hadn't retired a day too soon. See, old cops, ex-cops, retired cops, former cops, don't rate. When you're finished, you're finished. Even with your old pal Marinelli. Sure, he's still your old pal, but he's a cop and you're not, and that comes first with all of us, remember? So when you ask Marinelli about Gruber and company, he feels a personal obligation to you, but a professional obligation to me. See, as you know, I already realized what you might think, and I'd already asked Marinelli if you had any ene-mies, so when he called me right after you first walked into his office, I was ready for it."

"He called you?"

"Just to leave a message for you."

"I never got a message."

"I know, because it was really a message to me. Point is, you didn't tell Marinelli *not* to call me, did you? So his calling me with a message for you lets me know what you are up to without him being too disloyal to his old pal, see? After that, I had you on radar, every move you made—the undercover man, the little chat with Sergeant O'Dowd in headquarters, all of it."

"But why didn't you move on Gruber?"

"I did. I have. I'm here, aren't I? Even though I knew you were wasting your time. I've had an idea for a long time who killed Thompson. Someone a lot closer to home. I arrested him this morning. Then I got the message that you were talking to Gruber. *Again.*"

"You've actually got the guy?"

"I've actually got him."

"So what's with Gruber?"

"You're right. He's the chauffeur. Know who for?"

"That's what I've been trying to find out."

"The name Dougal mean anything to you?"

After a few seconds, Pickett said, "God Almighty. He's the worst."

A nurse appeared at the table. "Are you two the policemen here about the patient on the fifth floor? He's asking for you."

NINETEEN

PICKETT SAID, "Colin Dougal. I put him away. Convicted of assault. He beat up a pal of his and left him for dead. It was the second offense. He got seven years. When he came up for parole, after he'd served about three weeks it seemed like, they asked me, and I recommended he should serve every day of the rest and then some, but they must have let him out a little early. He's a menace, out of control, and he'll wind up a lifer sooner or later, after he's killed a couple more people. I suppose when they did what I recommended, he found out who had suggested it, and because of me, he stayed inside for a few more years than he might have. So when they let him out eventually, he came looking for me. His parole officer is a fed so he didn't report to the Bail-and-Parole Unit. That's how I missed him, missed noticing he was out."

Wilkie said, "While we're still here, let me tell you the rest of my story." And he told Pickett about Sproat's confession. "I thought I had it wrapped up, but this Dougal sounds like a loose cannon."

"We'd better hear Gruber's story," Pickett said.

"You do it, would you? You seem to be on his wavelength."

They entered the room to find Gruber lying at a

slight incline, his functioning eye still bright red but marginally more open now. The area around the eye, however, like much of the rest of his face, had turned deep black and purple.

Pickett and Wilkie sat beside the bed, and Wilkie reminded Gruber of who they were.

"I know who you are, for fuck's thake. I told them to fucking get you," Gruber said to Pickett.

The lisp nullified the aggression, making the swear words sound childish.

"Uh-huh. Why?" Pickett asked.

"Don't you want to know?"

"What?"

"About why I wath up there near that fucking cabin."

"Oh, that, sure. We know that. You drove up a guy who wants to kill me, right?"

Gruber's head twisted from Pickett to Wilkie as he took this in. "You want to know who?"

"We know that, too. Colin Dougal," Wilkie said. "Now, if you'd told me that in the beer parlor, it might have been worth a couple of years off your sentence, but we've found out—the hard way—so you've missed your chance. The best thing you can do now is tell us everything else, just in case there's something we missed."

"He fucking knowth." Gruber indicated Pickett. "Ask him."

"I know you went up there looking for me," Pickett said.

"I wasn't looking for you. I was jutht the fucking driver. He didn't want to risk the highway patrol. He's on fucking parole. So, I drove him up there."

Pickett said, "Connie, a couple of points—"

"I told you. I had nothing to do with it. Nothing."

Pickett said, "You drove the guy who was trying to kill me. You call that nothing? I'll tell you what I call it. Being an accessory. And if you don't want to have a sudden relapse, you will start cooperating, like acting polite, okay? You stupid prick. They tell me you couldn't even play hockey. All you were ever good for was spearing the real players, the ones who could skate. You were a 'policeman,' they tell me, a thug, hired to beat up the good players on the other team. 'A goon,' the term should be. And you still are. Goddam stick boy for the bikers. Now. You agreed to take Dougal up to Larch River so he could kill me. Right?"

"He said he jutht wanted to find out if you were up there."

"How did he know I had a cabin there?"

Gruber tried to shrug.

Pickett said to Wilkie, "Make sure the door's closed." He turned back to Gruber. "Come on, for Chrissake," he roared, his face six inches from Gruber's. "We have to find your pal before he kills someone else. We haven't got all goddam week. How did he *know?*"

"He overheard it."

Pickett continued to shout. "Where?"

"In the lineup at the Bail-and-Parole Unit."

"So he told you what he'd heard and said, 'Drive me up there so I can kill him,' and now you try to tell me that you didn't have anything to do with it. Why, you goddam bag of pus—"

"He didn't have a gun or anything."

"Try this, Connie. The OPP—Sergeant Wilkie here—doesn't give a shit about Dougal. No one saw Dougal, see. They saw you. Half the town saw a broken-down has-been of a hockey player driving around asking where I lived. The sergeant here doesn't need Dougal. He's got you."

"I didn't even go in the cabin," Gruber squawked. "I waited in the truck in the road while the guy went walking along the road and went into the cabin. The light came on in the cabin and I got out of the truck and went to thee what wath happening, and a few minutes later, thomeone was beating on my horn. When I went back to the road, Dougal wath thitting in the truck waiting to go."

"He killed Thompson?"

"When I looked in the window, I could thee Thompthon lying on the floor."

"Dead?"

"I didn't go in. He wasn't moving."

"So. Mission accomplished, then. If we hadn't identified you right away, you might have got away with it. What happened next? How come Dougal tried to kill you?"

Gruber looked away.

Pickett said, "Bill Sikes' dog, that's what you were. Still are. Find the dog and you've found Sikes, right? Sikes tried to drown the dog, just like Dougal tried to kill you. You were stupid, as usual. You made the mistake of telling Dougal we were on to you, probably right after I talked to you in the beer parlor. Probably you even told Dougal you hadn't said anything about him. So he knew he still had time to shut you up. What a pathetic asshole you are. Did you think Dougal would be grateful?'' Pickett turned to Wilkie. ''How long will he get, Sergeant? Fifteen years? Twenty? If he tells us where to find Dougal, he might cut it down to twelve maybe?''

''I fucking told you everything, didn't I?'' Gruber whined, coming back to life.

''A little late, though. There's one thing you can do yourself some good with. Where is Dougal now?''

''He stays in a house on Eastern Avenue, near Broadview. Look for an old white pickup.''

''We know where he stays,'' Wilkie said. ''And we know the truck. What we want to know is if he's not there, where might we find him?''

''He drinkth at the Stairway,'' Gruber said. He looked to Pickett. ''Where you firtht picked me up.''

Pickett said, ''What's made you change your mind, Connie? First you were scared to tell us, now you're scared not to. You concerned about Dougal killing someone else?''

''Fucking right. *Me. I'm* next. I just realized I'm under arrest now, right? I sure hope tho. But that won't thtop Dougal. See, he doesn't know you know it's him you're after. That's the fucking stupidity of it. When you came after me firtht, in that bar, I told him afterwards that you didn't know anything about him. Chritht. So he figures that if he kills me, he's thafe.''

''Two birds with one stone. Stops you identifying him, and stops you blackmailing him.''

''I didn't try to blackmail him,'' Gruber said automatically. ''But when he came after me, I told him

I hadn't said anything. All the more reathon to kill me now, he said."

"He doesn't know you haven't kept quiet since, though," Wilkie said.

"But he's still got nothing to looth by killing me, has he? If you know he killed the guy in the cabin, it's no worse if he kills me, too, just in cathe you *don't* know. It's a win-win. And he'll step on that hard-on you've put on guard like he's a cockroach."

"We'll look after you."

"Oh, shit. *You?*" Gruber said. "*You* going to thtop Dougal?"

They left him there. Outside, while Pickett looked for a washroom, Wilkie talked to the guard, then had a long conversation on his mobile phone with the guard's boss.

When Pickett returned, Wilkie said, "We'll check out the Stairway, but just to be sure. He isn't going to sit around in a beer parlor, is he? No, I think that now we wait." It was five o'clock. The two men set out to look for some coffee. There was a Second Cup coffee shop inside the hospital.

"You planning to eat downtown?" Wilkie asked, hoping for company over dinner.

"Charlotte's cooking steak-and-kidney pie. Come back with me and have some."

"Steak and what?"

"Don't do that. Steak-and-kidney pie. Don't make out you haven't heard of it. I'm not talking about sheep's eyeballs or testicles or fillet of unborn octopus, for Christ's sake. I'm talking about a treat for anyone who wasn't born in baloney heaven. Never mind the kidneys. What are you going to do about me? I gather everyone knows what I've been doing. Shit, I feel like Alec Guinness in *Tunes of Glory*. Remember? 'Ye canna court-martial old Jock, can ye, laddie? I knew ye when ye were a wee bairn.' But you have to do something, I guess.''

"I've already done it.''

"What?''

"Anyone who asked has been told that we—the OPP—have hired you to get close to one of the suspects. Marinelli knows it's bullshit, but if you think about it, I had to get *him* off the spot you put him on, didn't I?''

Pickett thought about Wilkie's solution and felt the tension flow away. He had never expected Wilkie to throw the book at him, but to do nothing seemed too much. "It's your call, Abe,'' he said.

"I know that. I'm calling you safe.''

"You're doing a lot.''

"That's what my dad said.''

So he had Wilkie's father to thank for some part of his pardon, probably even for suggesting the idea. It wasn't a thing he would ever be sure of, though, because to ask the question would be to take away from Wilkie's gesture. He scrambled for a response that would cover all possibilities.

"He raised you right,'' he said. "Thanks. All the other threads tied up?''

"A few eyewitnesses would help. We got a lead on the gray Chevy.''

"Remind me.''

"You remember. One of the cars stopping outside your cabin that night was a gray Chevy. The woman who uses your trailer saw it; twice, she thinks. So we ran a little check just in case the driver bought some gas on a credit card. The gas station on the highway gave us a list of license plates that had used cards and we ran them through the computer.''

"And?''

"We came up with only three that weren't local. One of them was a gray Chevy owned by a rental company.''

"Who took it out?''

"A Brit. A tourist.''

"A lot of people stop to admire my cabin. For a Brit, it must look like a museum piece.''

"It *is* a museum piece. Anyway, this guy still has the car out, probably, as you say, touring around. We'll find him and talk to him—the patrols have his license number, but I would think that that takes care of the Chevy.''

Wilkie stood up. "I'm going to call on my dad before I eat. Wanna stop by?''

"Where is he?''

"At home. He's retired, like you.''

"I know that. We were buddies once, remember? I knew you when you were still sucking on a bottle.''

"It's what you do at that age. Anyway, he's at home, painting something. Why? Want to come and see him?''

Pickett shook his head. "Next time. What I meant was, where is home?''

"Leaside. They're still living in the same house. You need a ride somewhere?''

Pickett shook his head. "I'm at Bathurst and St. Clair. Out of your way. Nah. I'll take a walk through the Eaton Centre. Charlotte needs one of those plastic things for measuring spaghetti portions. The kind with the grooves. They haven't made it to Larch River yet.''

BUT INSTEAD OF driving out to Leaside, Wilkie pointed his car north to the Don Valley Parkway and from there, across to York University. Perhaps, he thought, his wife would be glad to see him and would join him for a coffee. A nice surprise. He did not phone ahead so as not to spoil it.

When he found her office, she was busy. He appeared in her doorway and she looked up; she did not immediately break into a smile of pleased recognition, as some wives would, or rear back in irritation like some others. Her reaction was somewhere in between, and not much to do with either. She treated his appearance as more or less normal, as if he worked only fifty feet away, while she waited to see what he wanted.

As he began to explain, the door behind her opened and the dean said, ''Can we get started, please?''

She picked a file off her desk and stood up. ''This is my husband,'' she said.

The dean came forward and offered Wilkie a squidgy little hand, and then Helen took Wilkie's elbow and led him to the door.

''Can't stop now,'' she said. ''See you Saturday.'' Then, as he walked away, she called him back. ''Give me a kiss,'' she said. He stood still while she kissed him, then wiped off the lipstick with a Kleenex before she turned back to the dean.

It reminded Wilkie of his mother, who used to spit on her handkerchief to wipe away the chocolate from around his mouth when he was too young to stop her.

TWENTY

"SO WE'RE CERTAIN NOW? It was this Dougal guy?" Copps asked when Wilkie told him the story at the station.

"So says Gruber, and he knew exactly how Thompson lay there after he went down. That's becoming the litmus test for me, because whoever killed him would probably not be certain what he looked like on the floor when the dust settled. Anyway, it was either Gruber or Dougal, and why Gruber? Yeah, it was Dougal."

"Then why have we got this chicken farmer in our jail?"

"Because he confessed, for Christ's sake. Remember? Have you been in to see him? Has he called for a lawyer?"

"He just wanted to see his minister. The minister told him to confess."

"To what? And how long has *she* been out there?" He jerked his thumb at the outer office.

"She came to town right after we did, and she's been sitting out there ever since. I didn't want her to talk to Sproat until you said it was okay. I don't know what her rights are, but I figured that if we're going to hear some stories, it'd be better if they didn't talk to each other first."

"What about Sproat?"

"He wants to cooperate, tell us the real story, he says. Again, I thought we'd wait for you. We're a bit shorthanded."

"When we're talking to him, hang on to this: Dougal, or Gruber, killed Thompson, no matter what Sproat says."

"There's another little complication just in." Copps picked up a fax and waved it toward Wilkie.

Wilkie continued to busy himself for the interview with Sproat. "What's it say?"

"Ready for this? Here goes. 'Suspect in Larch River homicide apprehended in Port Hope. Presently held here. Shall we convey to Lindsay?' "

"For Christ's sake. Give me that." He read it silently. Then, "Did you follow it up?"

"I called them. Here's the story. You remember the girl in the gas station who wrote down the number of the truck because he gave her a brand-new twenty? They found the truck. Two brothers near Port Hope own it. They operate a septic-tank cleaning business during the day. At night, they drive around looking for stuff to steal. So the number chimed and the local patrol checked them out. When the brothers heard what they were being questioned about, they got so scared they told the patrol what they had been doing.

"Seems they hit a place in Kinmount, and in the course of taking everything movable, they came across the emergency stash in a bedroom drawer: a couple of hundred in new twenties. They spent one of them at the highway gas station on their way down to the 401. They even showed them the loot, still in the barn. Better than that, we searched the rest of the buildings and came across a lot of other stuff, including the booty missing from the break-in at Larch River two weeks ago, to which they admitted.

"These guys are admitting to everything, they're so scared of being stuck with a homicide charge." Copps laughed out loud. "Poor bastards. Just going about their business, a little Friday-night enterprise they've got going and they fall into this. It's a coincidence. Anyway, we've already got enough suspects. Shall I tell the local detachment that?"

"No. Tell them we want to interview the suspects in connection with the robbery on our turf. Let's pick up the credit for getting the license number. It was our idea."

"That's better, Abe. Take it easy. You didn't fuck up."

"We found Dougal, didn't we? All we have to do now is lay our hands on him."

SPROAT SAID, "The minister persuaded me to tell the truth. He said the guilty would be punished more quickly that way. I don't think Mrs. Sproat is guilty of anything except anger. It must have been self-defense." He spoke out of a deep tiredness.

"Tell us your story. The real one."

Sproat nodded. "I will try to tell you just what happened. First, Thompson came to see us—to see Mrs. Sproat, I mean—with his claim. But it was more than that. He was using words like 'swindled,' so I kicked him out. Then Mrs. Sproat went to see the church lawyer, and he advised her to resist Thompson's claim, as she told you. But he also advised her that when the matter came to court, if it did, there might be testimony from Thompson to support his claim, testimony of a kind she would find distressing.''

Wilkie was uncomprehending, and Sproat had difficulty elaborating. Copps interjected: ''Did the church lawyer think Thompson might claim that he had had sex with your wife?''

''Yes. It might be made to seem that Thompson and Mrs. Sproat had been living as husband and wife for some time, which would account for the low wages.''

''This upset your wife, of course.''

''She said it made her feel sick that such things might be said, especially in a courthouse. So on Friday night when I came home and found her away, I thought she might have gone to have it out with Thompson, and I drove to the cabin to calm her down. But I was too late. When I got there, Thompson was dead. I saw the piece of dowel and thought to remove it because it would have her fingerprints on it. When I came back to the farm, Mrs. Sproat was still away, but she came in shortly after. She said she'd been to see the minister, and now she did not want any mention of Norbert Thompson again. I wondered if she realized he was dead, but then I thought if he is, it was an accident, and I said no more until you found that piece of wood in the truck.''

''You confessed to save your wife?''

''Yes. No. I must be honest. I thought that when she realized what I was trying to do for her, she would speak up right away. I don't know why she hasn't. She must be confused.''

Wilkie nodded to Copps to carry on. Copps said,

"Tell us exactly what Thompson looked like on the floor."

"He looked dead!"

"How was he lying? Tell us."

Sproat did so, exactly.

"I don't think your wife is confused. She's clear about one thing: She didn't kill Thompson, she didn't even hit him. She may be confused about why you did, and didn't tell her."

"Me?" The amazement was deep and clear. "Me? I didn't kill Thompson. I was just—"

"We know. We know who did."

"Who?"

Wilkie shook his head. "We need to talk to your wife. Without you present. Now, we can charge you with withholding evidence and keep you here, but I'd just as soon we worried about that later, if we have to, so in the meantime, would you stay here until we've talked to your wife? Voluntarily? I'll leave the door open."

"Is my wife here?"

"She's been here all the time, waiting for you. When I send her in, you can go home, both of you. First we have to talk to her."

"I WAS SICK to my stomach at what the lawyer said, so I went out to the cabin to talk to Norbert. I wanted to ask him if he was going to say those things our lawyer said he might. Things the whole church would hear about. But he never had any idea of saying anything like that. That was lawyer talk."

"What *was* his idea?"

"He was disappointed. Mr. Maguire had promised him he'd leave a will deeding half the farm to him, for having looked after him these last few years."

"Did Mr. Maguire think maybe you would take up with Thompson after he was gone?"

"I never gave him any reason to think anything like that. I never thought anything of Norbert. He was too backward. But he had a home with us for as long as he liked. He knew that, yet I think he was told to move out."

"Who by?"

"By his lawyer. Or his girlfriend. Did you know he had a girlfriend? He did, though. In Sweetwater. They were planning to get married and move into the farm. He said I could stay. On my own farm! But then when Mr. Sproat turned up, Norbert saw there was no place for me and Mr. Sproat, as well as him and his girlfriend. So someone got to talking to him about his rights, and that's when it all started. I talked to the minister; he said we hadn't paid Norbert enough and that the farm had done well, so I became of a mind to pay Norbert something, enough to start his own place with, but the church lawyer said to wait until we were sure Norbert wasn't going to go any further."

"Did you tell Thompson this?"

"Yes, I did—when he told me at the cabin that he had no idea of saying dirty lies about him and me in court. He just wanted to be treated right, and I was always willing to do that."

"Did you get into an argument?"

"We started off that way, but once we got ourselves sorted out, and I said I'd help him as far as was fair, we shook hands and we went back to Sweet-water together, to see the minister. Norbert came with me to show the minister we had an understanding. The minister wasn't in, so Norbert walked home and I did some shopping and had a cup of coffee and waited some more, but the minister never showed up.''

"What did you want the minister for?"

"To ask him to tell the church lawyer that Norbert and I had got it sorted out, what we'd arranged.''

"Then you drove home, to the farm?"

"Yes.''

"Was your husband there?"

"Yes.''

"Did you tell him where you'd been?"

"I said I'd been to see the minister. When he asked a question, I said it was all sorted out and there was nothing more to discuss.''

Wilkie said, "Up at the farm, when Mr. Sproat said he'd done it, you didn't seem very surprised. Were you expecting something like that?''

"I was afraid. He's a very loving and protective man. You can't make it worse than that. It wasn't intentional.''

Copps looked at Wilkie, who once more nodded for him to go ahead. Copps said, "Your husband did go up to the cabin because he thought you might have gone there to have it out with Thompson. He found Thompson dead, so he thought you had killed him, and he hid that bit of wood to cover up for you. He couldn't just throw it away, though, because someone might recognize it, and it would have your finger-prints on it, and he hadn't had time to burn it.''

"My fingerprints? It never would—"

"We know. We're having it checked, and we think we know whose prints are on it. We already have him in custody. Point is, Mr. Sproat put it in the truck, under some sacks, and left it there too long."

"So he confessed to protect me?"

"More or less."

She nodded. "He would do that." Then, as the policemen stood up, she started to cry. "It was Mr. Maguire's fault really, then," she said.

Wilkie said, "Like your husband says, he was in a lot of pain, and he wanted to be sure you would be all right."

"He shouldn't have done it, though." She dabbed her eyes. "Poor Norbert. It wasn't his fault at all, was it? What about his girlfriend? Will she be all right?"

"She'll be all right."

"I might want to do something for her."

"You should speak to your minister about that first. Right now, why don't you take Mr. Sproat home? You could both do with a rest."

TWENTY-ONE

WHEN THEY HAD GONE, Copps said, "Where do you guess Dougal is now?"

"I know exactly where he is, or rather, I know where he will be soon. I've taken off the guard outside Gruber's hospital room."

When Copps understood this, he said, "Jesus, Abe, you want Dougal to kill him?"

"That would suit everybody. No. I want him to try. I've told the guard to stay inside the room with Gruber. I've set up a little trap, baited with Gruber. There are four plainclothes guys staking out the corridors leading to Gruber's room. If Dougal goes after Gruber, we'll catch him."

"And you think Gruber is right? That Dougal *will* come after him?"

"Just in case he doesn't, I've also got every other cop in Toronto looking for him. He's well known. We'll get him."

"What happens if he comes up here?"

"Why would he?"

"Because he's a psychopath. Because he's got Pickett on his brain."

"I've got a car watching Mel's house, and another one on Duck Lake Road watching the cabin. I'm playing it very safe."

"Good. Hello. Look who's here. I'll be outside if you need me."

Wilkie swung around and saw Helen standing in the doorway. He got up, alarmed. "Something wrong?"

She came quietly into the room and sat down in the chair Copps had vacated. "Am I interrupting? I went home first, but when you weren't there, I thought I'd, well, come here."

He waited for her news, which had to be dire to make her leave the university so suddenly. He asked her again, "What's wrong?"

"After you came by, I decided I wanted to go home for a bit. I told the dean I had to take some time off."

"I was just passing. What's wrong with dropping in to say hello, for Christ's sake? You don't want me to drop in? Okay. You just have to say so. Fine. I'll write and get permission before I do it again. Better yet, I won't do it again. Suits me. It's out of my way, anyhow."

"Please sit down, Abe. Of course if you're nearby, I want you to see if I'm free. It's me I'm having trouble with. I want to sort myself out. Because if I don't do it soon, there won't be anything left to sort out, will there?"

"Meaning?"

"You. I've never seen you looking so bleak as you did today."

"Was it that obvious?"

"Am I right?"

"I don't like the way we're living. I don't like being made to feel like a spare prick at a wedding when I call on my wife. I know, I know, that's the way women have always felt when they drop in at their husband's office at the wrong time. Maybe that's what I don't like. I thought about it all the way home. I still don't like it.''

"I realized today that things with you might have gone farther than I'd noticed. I don't want anything to happen that I'd be sorry for, just because we've let things drift.''

"I thought you had it all sorted out.''

"So did I, but it won't stay sorted out. You won't put up with it for much longer. I could see it in your face. And that frightened me. So I thought we should spend some time together and talk.''

"You've quit your job?''

"No, I *haven't* quit my job. After we've talked, that might be the thing to do. And it might not. The point is, I don't know. But if it's hopeless, I want us to decide, not just find out.''

"You're right about the main thing. After I left you today, I just about got to the point on the way home where I thought I would be making other plans.''

She didn't respond to that. After a few moments, she stood up. "Did you do anything about your dinner?''

"We could go to the Chew'n'Chat.''

"I'll see what I can pick up at the store.'' She stopped. "You are free, aren't you?'' Her voice was unsteady.

"I'll follow you up.''

Ten minutes later, he left. Copps did not look up as he passed.

HALF AN HOUR LATER, when Dougal stepped out of the bush beside Pickett's cabin, it was nearly full dark.

He had taken a chance on the highway patrol and borrowed a car from a supermarket parking lot; the white pickup, he knew, was just one more. He was on the 401 long before the owner came past the cashier, and just about in Larch River before the message about her stolen car had been distributed. And why would the OPP think a car stolen from a supermarket lot off Eastern Avenue was significant?

Dougal then made his way up to Larch River, crossed over the bridge in town and took the county road, turning onto the trail that led up behind the cottages on the other side of the river from Pickett's cabin. There he left the car and walked through the bush, following the river road until he came close to the clearing and came out behind the cabin. He had a whiskey bottle of gasoline in each hand, each bottle plugged with a piece of rag.

WHEN THE ALARM sounded, Wilkie was just finishing dinner with his wife. He was roused by the duty officer immediately—Pickett's cabin was now famous in Sweetwater—and he called Copps to meet him at the cabin.

He could see the fire almost as soon as he left Sweetwater, and he switched on all his emergency noise and lights to keep the sightseers from getting in his way. He met Copps coming down Duck Lake Road from the other direction, and the two cars almost collided as they pulled into the clearing. Pickett was waiting for them in the yard outside the trailer, his arm around a frightened Eliza.

Already the cabin was reduced to a glowing outline, and they stayed back, away from the heat, waiting for the fiery frame to collapse.

Pickett said, "Her boyfriend, Sarwin, went after him."

Eliza said, "There. In there. He went in there." She pointed and waved urgently at the bush on one side of the lot.

Pickett said, "Look after her, Wilkie," and made gestures of handing Eliza over to the sergeant.

Copps jumped forward, grabbing Pickett's arm, holding him back. "No, no. Fuck, no. *You* look after *her*. We'll look after these guys."

He indicated that Wilkie should follow him, and smashed into the wall of scrub, disappearing immediately. From behind him, Wilkie could see nothing, but he stayed close to the noise of the constable's progress. Copps, his forearms up to meet the willow branches that could tear his face open, finding some kind of trail under his feet, moved forward quickly. Then he stopped, holding on to Wilkie as the sergeant nearly stumbled into him.

"Listen," he said. There were shouts, and the noise of splashing water. "What is that?" he asked. "The river? So close?"

Wilkie, unable to tell if it was blood or mucus or tears or all three smearing his face—something had smacked him hard across the eyes and nose—tried to remember the first time Pickett had given him a tour of the lot. "It's a beaver pond, or an otter pond," he said. "A small one. Shallow."

They listened again. From the direction of the pond came the shouts of two men, and the noise of splashing. "Let's go," Copps said.

Once more Wilkie fell in behind as Copps kicked his way through the brush and this time, within ten yards, they came to the clearing and a pond illuminated by starlight, where two creatures, covered in mud and up to their waists in water, were trying to drown each other.

Copps launched himself at the pair, caught the one he wanted by the neck and dragged him up to the bank, where Wilkie was waiting with his gun out. An exhausted Gupta followed Copps out of the pond and flopped onto the bank.

"YOU DON'T GIVE UP easy, do you?" Pickett asked.

"You sonofabitch. Next time," Dougal said.

"There isn't going to be a next time. Gruber told us the whole story. He'll tell it again in court to get a couple of years off his own sentence."

"Gruber ain't going to tell the court anything. He's dead." Dougal looked at Wilkie. "Can we get this over with? Fuck standing here talking." He turned back to Pickett. "It was a mistake, killing that guy in the cabin. I wasn't after him."

"I know that. You were after me."

Copps had now wiped most of the heavy mud off himself, and Wilkie handed Dougal over to him and two other constables. As they drove off, Wilkie called headquarters to find out what had happened to Gruber. He listened, slipped the phone back on its rest and said, "Very simple. When Dougal saw all the guards I had posted, he created a little diversion. He got a hold of an orderly's uniform and set off the fire alarm. In all the confusion, when Gruber's guard poked his head out, Dougal sent him down the hall to hold the elevator while he 'prepared' Gruber to be evacuated. I suppose Gruber was hooked up to some of those bottles on wheels. When the guard came back to see why they hadn't come, he interrupted Dougal trying to strangle Gruber, who is back in intensive care, but he's still alive, for which I guess we should all give thanks. So that's that, and you were right, Mel.''

"We all were. And lucky. You going back to Sweetwater?"

"I have to book this character. Then I'm going home. My wife's there, waiting for me.''

"I WAS WATCHING HIM through the window of the trailer. I was just about to go out and ask him if he was lost—you know how slow one can be to respond to the unusual. I mean, if you saw Napoleon in the front garden, you would think, for a long time, 'He looks familiar,' so I wondered why he was in the yard. Then he lit the first of those Molotov cocktails he was carrying and threw it at the cabin. He watched it burn for a few moments, which gave me time to come to my senses and go out the door after him before he could throw the second one at us. He got it lit, then I was on him, so it just went into the bush. I suppose the bush is still too wet to catch, and the gasoline burned out. I assume that's what happened, because by then, I was chasing him through the woods. He had several seconds' start—twenty perhaps—but I had the advantage that he had to break the trail and I could follow more quickly." Gupta smiled. "I also had the advantage that I'm harder to see in the dark than he is. When he reached the pond and decided to go across it, then I had him, stuck in the mud. It was difficult because he wouldn't stand still long enough for me to get a proper grip on him, so I was glad when you arrived." Gupta smiled again to show he was joking.

They were sitting around Charlotte's table, where they had come once they had seen the embers of the cabin safely doused. The fire department had arrived in time to water the ruins and damp down the scrub around the clearing, but not in time to save the structure or anything in it.

Most of Larch River had come to watch the fun, and one of the bystanders had provided a clue as to why Dougal had returned, even though he must have learned from Gruber that Pickett was no longer using the cabin. The assistant in the hardware store, identifying the principals of the drama for the latecomers, but still misinformed, was heard to point out Eliza with the words, "That's his granddaughter; she stays in the trailer."

Wilkie, hearing this, made sure Dougal was well on his way to Sweetwater before he told Pickett, who had reacted—as Wilkie guessed he might—by looking around for Dougal so he could kill him.

Now Pickett had a second reaction. "Imogen," he said. "She'll surely be here any day. And my son. I'll have to drive in tomorrow." He turned to Charlotte. "I'll stay there until they come."

He didn't want Charlotte around when his son arrived. The man had said he had information, and

Pickett feared what that information might turn out to be.

Gupta said, "I am sorry about your cabin, Mel. Eliza has told me all about it. I understand what it meant to you, recreating the world of your pioneer ancestors."

"I can do it all over again now, can't I? Give me something to do in my old age."

"Really? You will build it again?"

"No."

"Perhaps it wouldn't be quite the same. The original achievement was so much like that of the first pioneers, when you had to work it out a step at a time. But now that you know how, it's just building a cabin, isn't it?"

"I feel like I'm being interviewed on CBC. Yes, it is."

"It would be a pity, though, if—"

"Sarwin," Eliza said.

He stopped, looking at her. "Yes?"

She held a finger to her lips. "Time to go."

AND THEN, late the next afternoon before he left, Pickett got a call from his neighbor in Toronto. His sister-in-law, Verna, was now in his neighbor's living room, demanding the keys to his house on the grounds that Pickett was dead and she was the closest relative, or her son was. Hope had sprung again in her breast; apparently the break with her had been so clean she had not heard that he had remarried.

He remembered the famous line from Mark Twain, or somebody: "'Tell her the news of my death has been greatly exaggerated,' Pickett said and then, satisfied, denied himself any further satisfaction. "Maybe not," he said. "Put her on."

"Who is this?" Verna's voice, even in three syllables, shrieked and rattled in his ear like a badly fitting cutlery drawer being closed. Abraham Lincoln said that every man over forty is responsible for his own face; now Pickett thought that every woman over fifty is responsible for her own voice. Verna sounded like the Wicked Witch of the East. Appearances are not deceptive, he thought, wondering if it was not time to buy himself a little notebook to write down such thoughts. He reckoned he thought something interesting like that four or five times a year; one little notebook would last him.

"Are you there?" she squawked.

"This is me, Verna."

"What are you playing at? We heard you were dead."

"No, I'm alive. Here in Larch River. Sorry."

"Don't be funny with me, Mel Pickett."

"Thanks for wanting to help out, Verna. But, you know, Charlotte, my new wife, she would have let you know."

A considerable silence followed. "Your new *wife!* I can rely on that, can I? Where did you find this one? Jarvis Street?" It was no more than an attempt to try for an aggressive response to the fairly shattering news, but it made Pickett angry at last.

"What difference does it make?" he asked.

"No skin off my nose, but a friend of mine was telling me recently that Harvey has considerable status as far as family estates are concerned. Has to do with reasonable expectations of having a valid claim on an estate.''

What Pickett had always feared was that somewhere there existed the evidence of his ''son's'' true parentage, which would come to light after his death and create a huge muddle should Charlotte die before him, or at the same time, say in a car crash. Blood tests might be used to disprove his parentage of his son. DNA, by Christ. He was hearing now that Verna would try anything. She had to be sent on her way.

''Yeah? As far as I'm concerned, Verna, old dear, the expectations of your son come a long way behind the claims of my wife, my granddaughters, my son, and any other connections they might have. Don't get your hopes up. I'll check it out, though, make sure it's watertight; you've obviously been talking to a lawyer, but don't let him charge you too much. You haven't a hope, according to my lawyer.''

''You bugger, Mel Pickett. But maybe it won't all be in your hands. Maybe this new wife has a shred of decency in her.''

God Almighty. Now Verna was announcing that if all else failed, she planned to hound Charlotte, and probably Imogen, too. ''Well, good luck,'' was all he could think of that he wouldn't regret later. He needed some time to figure out how to dispose of her for good. ''Let me speak to my neighbor again.''

Pickett apologized for putting his neighbor in the cross fire, and told her not to give his keys to Verna under any circumstances.

Then she said, ''There's someone else here. An Englishman.''

''Who? What's his name?''

Now the man spoke. "This is George Colwood. You know?"

"Jesus! What are *you* doing there?"

"I arranged to meet your sister-in-law here when I heard you were dead."

"How did you know where to find her?"

"I phoned the police, and the clerk said she was listed as your next of kin."

"That computer's out of date." But the news muddled his attitude to Verna. To know she was still listed somewhere as his next of kin was to have provided her with some hope. Not all her fault.

Colwood continued. "She told me your neighbor had a key, and she drove down from Hamilton to meet me here."

"*Up* from Hamilton, not down. But now she knows there's no reason for her to stay. I'll hang up now and you can tell her I'll be meeting you there, alone, later on. When she's gone, call me back. Hang on, hang on. Does she know who you are?" Pickett feared that his son had discovered his true parentage and had already told Verna.

"Well, no. No. I, er, didn't think it was necessary to broadcast it. I have explained to, er, friends and others that I'm visiting you from England. A family acquaintance from the war."

Pickett silently offered thanks to the English practice of never telling anyone your family's business, not even other members of your own family. "Kick her out, then," he said cheerfully. "Then call me back. But stay mum about us—you and me."

The phone rang forty-five minutes later. Verna had

been hard to get rid of, but finally Pickett was alone on the telephone with his son.

"Can you wait for me?" he asked. "I'll be there in a couple of hours."

"Of course. Your neighbor is making us a cup of tea."

"Is Imogen there?"

"Not at the moment. She's off to look at the shops. She says everything is half price in Canada. She'll be here when you arrive."

"I'm leaving now."

"Shall I wait here? It seems like an imposition on your neighbor. You're going to be rather late."

"Let me speak to her. I'll tell her to give you the keys; you can make yourself at home."

TWENTY-TWO

"SO YOU JUST CAME to check me out?"

"To see if I wanted to be connected. To you. I thought I had the right to choose. When I was finished in New York, I decided I would scout around a bit first, so I drove up to Larch River on Friday to look at this cabin that Imogen has been talking about. She said you would have moved up there by now. I found the cabin and peeked through the window, but the man I saw didn't fit Imogen's description of you, so I waited in the road for a few minutes wondering what to do, then drove to a place called Fenelon Falls and found an inn. I returned to Larch River in the morning. I was having a cup of coffee in the motel coffee shop when I heard the news. I gather it's not true."

"I'm not dead yet, no." Pickett walked to the window. "That your car parked out there?"

"A gray Chevrolet? Yes."

Pickett said, "How long were you waiting on the road by my cabin?"

"Not long. A few minutes."

"Did you see anyone else coming or going?"

"A woman in a little sort of farm lorry…"

"A pickup truck."

"That the term? As I left, before I reached the end of the road, I saw her turn into your drive. I waited a bit more, then she drove out with the man I had seen through the window. That was all.''

Pickett made a mental note to tell Wilkie that he had some confirmation of the Sproats' story if he needed it, if Dougal should clam up before they got a statement signed.

But he was wondering now how to proceed with his visitor. On the drive down from Larch River, he had been over it again and again, seeking the self-justifying thread that could be spun into a lie, whatever came out. Once upon a time, he had been gallant, and that should have been the end of it, but now, after all this time later, why was the fiction continuing? Pickett scrambled to remember a justification and found it in his duty to continue to protect the man who was Imogen's real grandfather, a respectable married teacher of art in a secondary school, who, in 1945, would have been ruined if the truth had come out.

And now? Who knew? The man might now be a bishop, and perhaps the liberated times would turn against him and he would be condemned for having been a coward back then. There. See? Pickett couldn't risk upsetting a man's life, could he? Thus he tried to prepare for his son's announcement of his discovery.

He had tried to keep the initiative when he arrived. ''We can be formal,'' he'd said. ''Or we can use first names, which is probably more common over here than with you. What I'd find real awkward, at this stage, is you calling me 'Dad.' Okay?''

His son was a slightly built, handsome man of less than medium height, with thinning fair hair and a still watchfulness that kept his features from expressing anything. He was wearing a tweed suit and brogues, an outfit of a quality that even Pickett recognized represented the income of a very successful man. When he spoke, there was a tiny speech impediment to do with the letter "r," but hardly detectable within the English accent. "I'd find it awkward, too. *Very awkward.*" He drew in his breath, waiting to be asked what he meant.

Pickett sensed the ticking of the bomb. "You said you'd heard something, or found out something, about you and me?" Now he was sure of what he was going to hear.

Colwood waited for a few seconds to give his words their full weight. "Do you remember my Uncle Ernie? My mother's brother?"

"No. Yes. I met him just once. A wireless operator in the RAF, right? Nice guy."

"A decent bloke. We never saw much of him, but a solid type."

And now Pickett knew the form the discovery had taken. Ernie, long forgotten, was the only one in the family who knew the truth. His sister had confided in him at the time so that he would not be tempted to get a couple of pals and teach Pickett a lesson for seducing his sister, possibly by putting on ammunition boots and waiting for him outside the pub, the lower-class equivalent of a horsewhipping. Ernie had come to Pickett then to let him know that although the family officially regarded Pickett as a rotten bastard, he, Ernie, knew different, and wanted to thank Pickett for looking after his sister.

"I remember Ernie," Pickett sighed. "I thought I could trust him."

"You could. But you must know what *I've* thought of you over the years. The man who poked my mother and then wouldn't marry her. A Grade-A bastard. Uncle Ernie could have set me straight long ago and saved us all a lot of trouble."

"I've thought about that," said Pickett, slowly gathering his wits. "I don't know if it would have made it easier for you. Why did he tell you, finally?"

"When Imogen wrote and said she'd tracked you down and was staying with you, I got alarmed. I had no idea she was coming over here to look for you. Well, yes, she said something about it, but I didn't think she had a hope of finding you, or of getting you to meet her if she did. When she did both, I wanted to fly over myself. I didn't want her mixed up with a man I regarded as a royal shit, no matter what my mother said."

Pickett said, "Your mother didn't agree?"

"She would never hear a word against you. Anyway, Uncle Ernie took me aside when he heard I was coming over. He has cancer and thought it was time to tell me what was what. Why didn't you tell Imogen the truth?"

Pickett didn't even bother to answer this question. He had had time to think. "Did Ernie tell you who your father was?"

"No. Mother wouldn't tell him."

"So, since it wasn't me, you were left wondering who your real father was. And your mother went through a lot to protect him."

"So did you, of course." Colwood seemed to be losing a bit of his attitude now that the human factor, the real Pickett, had appeared.

"I was nineteen," Pickett said. "I enjoyed being able to help your mother. And then when Imogen turned up, I wasn't sure I had the right to tell her the truth. You still haven't told her, have you? See? It's a problem. Her grandmother trusted me; her real grandfather was very respectable. Why *haven't* you told Imogen?" Pickett began to relax. The hell with it, he thought. Let them know it all. Let them get on with it.

Colwood said, "I thought I would have it out with you first. Why didn't you tell her when she first arrived?"

Pickett fought to construct his response. The reality had been that telling Imogen would almost certainly have involved telling his colleagues, and he was simply not up to it. And once he had met Imogen, he didn't want to, anyway.

Gradually his brain stopped trembling as an idea took on a form. "It was a problem. You realized that or you would already have told her yourself. As I said, your mother's lover—your father—was a very respectable man." Pickett was mentally clearing his throat, almost ready to begin. First, he went on to the reasons how, in 1944, a man in the lover's position could be destroyed.

"You know who it was?" Colwood demanded.

"Yeah. Yeah, I know."

"I think I'm entitled to know. He's my father."

"All right, then. And afterward, could we talk about what you will do with the information?"

Colwood gave him a bitter glance. "Ever since I was old enough to understand, I've thought my mother was seduced by some Canadian shit. Now I might want to tell the real shit what I think of him.''

"And you might not be able to. But I'd like to be the one to tell Imogen. Okay?''

Colwood shrugged. "So what's his name? He's probably dead by now.''

Pickett took the first step, finding a plausible, English-sounding name. "Does Derek Hanstead mean anything to you?''

"No.''

"Art teacher.'' That was safe enough.

"No.''

"He died about six years ago. He had moved after the war, and was a teacher at a girls' school in Yorkshire somewhere. On the moors. He never married, but after he died, his house was sold and the new owner dug up the back garden and found the skeleton of a woman.''

Colwood went white. "Who? Who was it?''

"Turned out to be a colleague of his who had gone missing thirty years before. Her skull was fractured in three places.''

"A teacher?''

"So I understand.''

"He killed her?''

"They think so. He certainly buried her.''

"Dear God.''

Pickett feared he had gone too far, too soon. "I'm sorry I had to tell you. I'll look after telling Imogen.''

"You aren't going to tell Imogen this!''

"I have to, don't I? Isn't that why you came?''

"But bloody hell, this makes a lot of difference. Can we think about it for a minute?''

"I've been thinking about it for fifty years."

"Yes, I see." Colwood leaned forward, the mask of his face dissolving as he lost his last threads of detachment from Pickett. He squeezed his hands between his knees, like a boy. His white face was patched with red on the cheekbones, giving him a hectic, fevered air. "I say, could you, could we, have a cup of tea? Or coffee, if that's all you have."

"I've got tea. Would you like a drink, though? Scotch?"

Colwood shook his head, then thought for a moment and nodded. "Both. Make a cup of tea, if you would, but I'd like a scotch now."

With the scotch gone, and sipping his tea, Colwood said, almost as if to himself, "It's a lot to absorb, isn't it? What am I going to do?"

"Ready for more?" Pickett asked.

Colwood looked frightened, but nodded.

"I made it up," Pickett said. "I've no idea of where your father is now, or if he's alive."

"You made it *up!*"

"I wanted to lay out one possibility before you ran off to tell Imogen."

Colwood watched him, looking for a way to attack.

Pickett continued. "Once upon a time I did something when I was a kid because I loved your mother, and she loved someone else and she got pregnant by him. It was easy to let go, and stayed easy until Imogen came looking for me. I wasn't ready for that. If I had known she was coming, I'd have made sure I was out when she arrived."

"But why didn't you just tell her the truth?"

"First of all, think about what it would have looked

like to my mates. They would have assumed she was my granddaughter and that I was being a bit of a prick not to acknowledge her. There was no way I was going to tell the whole world the truth. I might have once, but not after fifty years. And then there's Imogen. Once I'd met her, I wanted to keep her. All right? She looks like her grandmother.''

''I know you are fond of her. She is of you. I wondered a bit about that.''

Pickett let this go by.

''Now what?'' Colwood asked when Pickett failed to respond.

''Maybe your uncle should have kept quiet. Then you could have come over here and bawled me out like you wanted to. Now it's your problem.''

''Mine?''

''Sure. Now that you know, it's all yours, and I'm very glad of it. I'm tired of it. I was soft on your mother fifty years ago, so I covered for her. Now there's Imogen, and you, and my goddam sister-in-law.'' Pickett explained how the plan to adopt Colwood had grown out of a need to protect his estate against Verna's greed. ''See, I couldn't help thinking of Imogen as my granddaughter once I'd met her, and everything followed from that. You are a man of the world—that the term?—so take some advice. Consult your company's lawyers. I don't think lawyers *should* get involved myself, except to draw up the adoption papers, but do what you like, George. George? That right? Just let me know what you plan to do. I'd like to get it settled. And if you decide to tell the truth, I want to tell Imogen myself. And that will probably be that. But if you go home first…oh, fuck it. Do what you like.'' He turned and moved quickly to the kitchen and poured a glass of water. When he came back, he was composed.

Colwood seemed smaller. He nodded at the offer of a refill, waited until Pickett was seated, then said, ''I'm sorry. When Ernie told me, I was already booked for New York. Then I thought I'd try to meet you and find out from you who my real father was. But now, with you and Imogen so close...I need time to think.''

''The more time you take, the harder it will be to tell Imogen the so-called truth and explain why you waited so long to tell her. You'll be in the same position I'm in now.''

Colwood looked at him over his glass. ''No one else knows?''

''No. All I know is that your father was a married man, an art teacher, and I'm the only one who knows even that much, except for you now.''

''Then let's leave it alone.'' Colwood looked as if he had decided to ignore a discrepancy in a major client's accounts for the sake of a larger good, like the security of the realm. A huge decision.

''Permanently?''

Colwood shook his head. ''I can't say that. I don't know what to do at this moment, so I don't want to do anything. But that could change.''

''It worked for fifty years.''

''I just can't promise.''

Pickett said, ''But you'll let me be the first to know, won't you?''

''No news will always be good news.''

"So I'll carry on, shall I, as the Canadian shit who seduced your mother?"

"Yes, well, sorry about that. But we can all take Imogen's word for it that you're not such a shit, can't we?" He tried to smile. "Why not?"

Pickett said, "Now let's get ready for Imogen when she comes back. How am I supposed to act with you, now we've met?"

Colwood said, "Now that we've met, we're getting along fine, surely. She would expect that to happen, because she likes us both." Colwood scrambled to make common cause with Pickett. "By the way, Imogen wants to come back to Canada to live for a while. Her sister thinks she might like to visit her here. I refused to talk about it before I left, but...how would you feel about it? If we carry on as is, I mean."

"Her sister can stay with Imogen. Upstairs. Imogen can have Grandad to dinner to meet her. And Grandma, too."

Colwood said, "I thought your wife—"

"I got married again. I didn't write to Imogen about it yet."

Colwood wiped his nose with a handkerchief. "Perhaps I should stay and meet my stepmother. What's she like?"

Pickett blinked. "She's presentable enough when she remembers to wear her shoes."

"What?"

"You're asking me what my wife is like. What kind of question is that? You want to know whether your stepmother is suitable for Epsom society?"

"No, no. Oh, no. I'm sorry if I gave that impression. No. Please. You must think I'm a real idiot."

Pickett said, "Let's put it back in the box. Now. You can meet my wife the next time you're over."

"As you like. I'd be happy to stay for a day or so if you thought I should."

"There's no need. What are you going to say at home, in England?"

"I'll tell them we met, got along well, but didn't have much in common."

"So you'll stop going around Epsom calling me a shit?"

"All right, all *right*. I'll change my tune now I've met you. Sshsh." He held up a hand.

The front door opened and Imogen came in, shouted with glee, embraced her grandfather, and kissed her father. She glanced at the cups and glasses and said to her father, "See? I told you. What's the matter, Dad? You look upset. Aaaaah." She put her arms around him. "Reunions."

Colwood said, "We've had a good talk, and now I have to go." He tried for a joke. "You have my permission to know him," he said to Imogen, kissed her, shook hands with Pickett and said, "Please give my regrets to your wife. Tell Imogen who I mean." And then, too many emotions coursing through him, he moved quickly to the door. "Call me at the hotel tomorrow morning, Imogen. I'll try to fly out tomorrow night, but you might want to stay over for a day or two. Let me know."

"WHAT WAS THAT all about?" Imogen asked when her father had left.

"We were talking about your grandmother. And speaking of grandmothers, I have something to tell you. Let's go out for some spaghetti. This is serious. It's about your new grandmother. I'd like you to come up to Larch River to meet her. We could go up tomorrow, come back the next day.''

One day, he thought, Colwood's curiosity would overcome him and he would try to find out who his true father was, but by that time, Pickett would be dead, surely, and Colwood would almost certainly get nowhere with his inquiries. The story would eventually become a family legend, and one day someone would turn it into a novel, perhaps.

Then the truth would come out.

HARLEQUIN®
INTRIGUE®

WE'LL LEAVE YOU BREATHLESS!

If you've been looking for thrilling tales of
contemporary passion and sensuous love stories
with taut, edge-of-the-seat suspense—then
you'll love Harlequin Intrigue!

Every month, you'll meet six new heroes
who are guaranteed to make your spine tingle
and your pulse pound. With them you'll enter
into the exciting world of Harlequin Intrigue—
where your life is on the line
and so is your heart!

THAT'S INTRIGUE—
ROMANTIC SUSPENSE
AT ITS BEST!

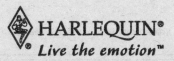

HARLEQUIN®
Live the emotion™

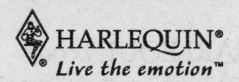
HARLEQUIN®
Live the emotion™

Upbeat,
All-American Romances

flipside

Romantic Comedy

 Harlequin Historicals®

Historical,
Romantic Adventure

INTRIGUE

Romantic Suspense

HARLEQUIN®

HARLEQUIN ROMANCE®

The essence of
modern romance

HARLEQUIN®
Presents

Seduction and passion
guaranteed

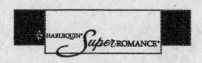

Emotional,
Exciting, Unexpected

Sassy, Sexy, Seductive!